GW00580078

Do not look backward when Running forward,

Do not look downward when flying upward.

# Contents / 目　录

# Contents / 目　　录

### 1. A Tender Mother

The sky was gray and cold signaling an impending heavy rain. A black car drove alone on a narrow and potholed road. From dusk until nightfall the car kept going. The driver turned on the headlights to dispel the darkness of the wilderness.

Julia sat in the middle of the back row staring at the road illuminated by the headlights. There was silence all around: only the sound of car engines could be heard. Julia and her mother were seated next to another mother and daughter heading to Palm County for a dance competition.

Watching the fleeting shadows of the cypress trees around her, a feeling of isolation surged in Julia's heart. It seemed as if there were only the black car and its five occupants left in the whole world. She looked around as her mother stared at the road ahead. The driver was driving attentively. No one spoke a word.

A feeling of unexplained evil enveloped her. All kinds of bad signs about car accidents, robbery, and abduction flashed through her mind. She tilted her head on one side and glanced at her mother. Without showing any emotion Julia's mother was just staring at the road ahead. Julia held her mother's warm hands in both her small hands. Her mother turned with a smile on her face. At that moment, Julia felt comforted and much warmer. She played with the things on her mother's clothes, resting her head on her chest.

"Mom, how long will it take?" Julia looked into her mother's eyes and asked.

"Around two hours," her mother replied gently as always.

"I guess I'll be unable to complete my homework today. The teacher's assignment for the vacation."

"You can do it early tomorrow morning or after the competition ends."

Julia remained silent. She seemed depressed about the path ahead, worried by the 8th-grade homework in the trunk, and the uncertain results of the impending dance competition. She was incredibly clearheaded as the worries blasted away her sleepiness.

"Why do I always have endless homework?" Julia pondered in her heart.

She felt the cold air and saw the vast darkness outside the window, as if she and her mother had been abandoned by the world. She wanted to cry, but she held back her tears forcefully due to her shyness.

At the next dance competition Julia wore a pink national costume and a big red flower with a diamond-shaped sequin on her head. She performed a peacock dance for the organizing committee members and won the judges' recognition with her exquisite dancing skills, ultimately earning a second prize.

After the competition Julia and her mom sat in a cafe and enjoyed some banana pie. Although Julia had never tried it before she found the strange scent to be a little off-putting. She took a small bite and ended up giving the rest to her mother, who thoroughly enjoyed it. Suddenly, Julia felt a sense of boredom creeping in. She remembered the unfinished homework that awaited her and the strict attitude of her teacher. This dampened her appetite even further. She sat there, observing the people around her with a touch of anxiety in her melancholic gaze.

"Mom, when are we going home?" Julia pouted and asked her mother in a spoiled tone.

"I've got tickets for tomorrow," her mother replied, having finished the entire banana pie by now.

" So where should we go next?" Julia continued asking.

"Go buy something. The persimmon cakes here are famous. We can bring some back to the relatives."

Julia remained silent, still pouting. The acne on her face was visible. Since the age of 9, the year when she started learning to dance, she had been plagued by acne. Although it was called "acne", it was an allergic reaction to cosmetics due to frequent makeup for performances. For the sake of love and art, there was no choice but to sacrifice delicate skin. From that point on she never knew what it felt like to have smooth skin on her face. She despised her pockmarked skin, but her love for dance outweighed her concerns. Julia had realized early on that **the world's glory comes at a price. You have to sacrifice one thing to gain another.** Just as she loved to dance she had to accept the pain and boredom of practicing basic skills as well as the damage to her skin from stage makeup.

After several days of sleet, sunlight appeared outside the window. It was afternoon, the sun shone in the puddles of water on the road surface, the melting ice on the eaves and the snowy area on the street made the whole street look lovely. Seeing this excited Julia and the tightness in her brow finally stretched out a bit.

"Mom, let's go."

"Let's go."

Her mother paid the bill and took Julia out to catch a taxi to their destination, the farmers' market.

## 2. Where Did the Temple Go?

There has been a strange incident in the county recently. Some buildings often disappear strangely. For example, the temple that stood in the middle of the road yesterday suddenly vanished today. The yellow-walled temple seemed to have never existed; it had disappeared into thin air.

This incident not only alarmed the local police station but also caught the attention of the city government. The mayor sent a fact-finding mission and there was a bunch of journalists swarming around, trying to get the scoop. Everyone was perplexed as they wandered around the empty square. No one knew where such a large building had gone.

"Did you call the monks?" journalist Jon asked an old man on the street.

"Well, you know there's a rule in this temple that they refuse any electronic devices so the monks inside don't have phones and no one can contact them. Besides, in our county, there aren't any telephones at all.   It's underdeveloped here. But we are used to it, and it doesn't affect our daily lives," said the old man, with a smile.

"What?" Jon's tone was somewhat surprised. "Isn't it inconvenient without communication devices?"

"It's not a big deal, young man. You see, in our county the pace is slow and we don't have many modern devices. But the good thing is that the place isn't big, and no one is in a hurry. We produce and sell our own food and daily necessities locally. Besides, the locals don't have big aspirations, so they don't feel the need to improve their lives or have anything urgent to attend to."

Jon couldn't believe his ears. He turned the camera around and all he could see were buildings and modern architecture. It wasn't desolate. The street layout was even quite artistic and stylish, yet the old man said it was like an uninhabited ravine, rather than a modern county.

Suddenly, a deafening roar filled the sky. Jon glanced upwards, finding only a few leisurely white clouds in the bright and sunny sky. How could there be thunder on such a sunny day? Puzzled, he looked around but couldn't find an explanation. Determined to get some answers, he approached an old man nearby and asked,

"Does this happen frequently?"

The old man gave a mischievous and enigmatic smile as he replied, "Not really. It was something you happened to see today. According to our local beliefs, when thunder rolls like this it's the Dragon King passing by, bringing good tidings. You're fortunate to see it and maybe something good will come out in a while."

Just then another thunderous boom echoed through the air causing the journalist's ears to ring. He noticed a shadow briefly cast upon the once-clear sky. It seemed the old man's words held some truth; there were indeed objects in the sky. However, he couldn't blindly trust the old man's claims. Jon had been in the reporting field for many years and although he had encountered some extraordinary events he remained a pragmatist. Without witnessing the truth firsthand he could not bring himself to believe in supernatural occurrences. But the strange incidents he had recently discovered in Palm County had begun to challenge his skepticism. The mysterious disappearance of the temple, the thunder and shadows on a cloudless day, and the peculiar grin on the old man's face all sent a chill down his spine; yet they also ignited an insatiable desire for exploration and curiosity within him.

"If there truly are mysterious forces at play, this report will surely make headlines."

With this thought in mind Jon's interest was piqued and he decided to stay in the small town for a few more days until the truth behind these peculiar events was discovered.

### 3. The Beautiful Small County

Julia was getting impatient again. She watched her mother carefully picking fruits and vegetables at this market and once again felt bored. Being a 14-year-old adolescent she naturally tended to be hostile towards everything and resisted for no reason. She tugged at her mother's sleeve.

"Almost finished, Mom?"

"Be patient. Haven't you noticed how fresh the fruits and vegetables are here?"

Julia usually just focused on eating. She didn't have a concept of whether unprocessed fruits and vegetables were fresh. She glanced at the stalls and realized that the fruits and vegetables on these were indeed vibrant, large, firm and plump, almost like little talking chubby people. Julia looked up at the stall owners again and noticed that they were full of bright smiles. Their faces showed no signs of exhaustion or dust from the hard work of the fruit farmers in the market. Instead, they seemed as cheerful as retirees who had no worries about food and clothing.

"What do you like? I can give it to you," said a radiant female vendor to Julia.

Julia, with her usual wariness and shyness hid behind her mother while sneakily glancing at this woman. She was typically "a lion" at home.

"Come on! Say thanks to the aunt!" the mother said, looking at Julia behind her with a big smile. Then she turned to the stall owner and said, "Thank you, we will pay for it."

Julia looked around. It seemed like there was no such thing as bargaining at this farmers' market. Every stall owner was kind and friendly, and the buyers didn't try to take advantage either. Both parties conducted their transactions courteously.

It was afternoon. The sunlight outside hid behind huge white clouds, occasionally peeping through the cracks and casting sparse rays. The ice cone on the eaves was trickling down. Julia observed everything outside. The market was surprisingly quiet. She felt that everything seemed to be at a standstill, but suddenly, a warm and beautiful feeling welled up in her heart. She looked at the lovely brightness outside. The water in the small river flowed with a gurgling sound. Turning towards the interior the fruits and vegetables were neatly arranged and the vendors were polite and friendly.

"What a wonderful place!" Julia couldn't help but exclaim.

On their way to the station, after shopping with her mother, she couldn't stop thinking about the scene they had just witnessed at the market. She wondered if she had stumbled upon a hidden paradise. Excitedly, she shared her impressions with her mother who agreed that they had never encountered such friendly vendors and fresh fruits before.

The taxi driver dropped them off on the opposite side of the station. As they stepped out of the taxi and were preparing to check their tickets at the station they realized that they were not at the station at all. They had entered the entrance door pointed out by the driver only to find an empty lobby with no ticket inspection machine or any signs of a station.

They walked out of the door and discovered that the sign with the words "Palm County Station" was gone.

They couldn't believe what they were experiencing. They turned around, hoping to find the driver, but he had already left. Upon turning their gaze towards the station, they were astounded to find that the entire station had vanished.

## 4. Central Street of Palm County

Having been in Palm County for a week Jon still has no clue what was going on. He has been trying to get some breakthroughs with the local police, but they don't seem to care about this matter. They hadn't even put it on record. Instead, they were more interested in trivial matters like searching for lost cats or discussing whether the grapefruits on their trees had grown watermelon peels.

"There's so much exciting news in Palm County!" Jon thought. "Why have I never discovered such a magical and mysterious place before?"

The girls here are gorgeous, natural, and carefree. What's even more adorable is that they are not arrogant or conceited. They treat everyone kindly and warmly, communicating with sincere eyes.

You can't sense any calculations or lies in their clear eyes, nor do you see any sorrow or anxiety. This kind of beauty gives you a sense of feeling beautiful just by being yourself. It amazed Jon that every woman he met here possessed this quality. On the other hand, in his city he has never encountered such stunning women. The women in his city seem to have a certain agenda behind their beauty. When they are young they exude allure to entice men, but as they mature their eyes reveal complex emotions and a cold and indifferent demeanor similar to wild animals.

While Jon was sitting in the cafe and immersed in his thoughts he was suddenly attracted by the roar of a police car outside. He walked out of the cafe looking in the direction the police car was going and immediately started his car. He followed the police car to a square where some people were queuing, but there was nothing else there. After inquiring, it turned out that this used to be a train station. Some people saw the train station disappear at 3:33 that afternoon. A mother and daughter were the ones who reported it to the police and they were currently receiving comfort and investigation.

Jon walked over and saw the mother and daughter. The mother was beautiful and seemed gentle, probably a local woman. The daughter was a bit stubborn, but still very clear. While he was looking at the mother and daughter he discovered that the girl was also looking at him. Jon showed a friendly hand to greet the girl, but the girl just looked at him without talking, as if she had something on her mind.

After comforting the mother and daughter, the police settled them in a hotel next to the police station, but Jon felt worried, unsure of which building would disappear next. It seemed like the whole city had a disease that would cause the loss of buildings. It was the first time in his life that he'd heard of two buildings disappearing so he followed the police car and arrived at the hotel where the mother and daughter had settled.

After friendly communication the girl's mother    agreed to be interviewed.

"The little girl seems upset. Did she get scared?" Jon asked kindly.

He looked elegant and refined, with a gentle and friendly demeanor

"She has been thinking of her homework," the mother replied softly, "This kid is very motivated and has good academic performance."

"Oh, that's great. Congratulations on having such a wonderful kid with all her talents. I heard that she also won second prize in the dance competition this time."

The mother looked down at her daughter with a smile on her face and a light of pride in her eyes. "She's not satisfied yet. She said she didn't get first place."

"It's great, girl," Jon said with comfort. "There are plenty of opportunities ahead."

The girl's mouth closed, and she stared at Jon for a while. Suddenly, she burst into tears causing both adults to panic. Her mother hurriedly picked her up.

"Sweetheart, what happened? Are you scared?"

She gently caressed the girl's head with her warm hands.

"Mom, can we go home?" The girl said, sobbing.

"We'll be home soon. You see, the police officer and this big brother just came to help us."

"Yes, little girl. Don't worry. Now we will spend the night here. Tomorrow we can go to the bus station and buy a return ticket. We can go home by bus too, it's just not as fast as a train," Jon said.

Hearing the comfort of the two adults the girl began to choke and stopped crying intermittently.

Jon felt uneasy, thinking that the girl was not in the right state to be interviewed. So, he bade farewell to the mother and daughter and prepared to return to his lodging.

As he stood up and was ready to leave he heard the sound of a police car outside the hotel again. The hotel owner and several people with friendly faces stood at the door looking in the direction of the police car.

"What happened? Sir, what's the commotion this time?"

The boss looked at Jon and said calmly, "I heard that the bus station on the east side has suddenly disappeared and even the passengers who'd just entered."

Jon was greatly surprised. He opened his mouth wide, experiencing the feeling of shock for the first time that left his jaw dropped. He turned around and looked at the girl, but this time she didn't cry.

"Now this mother and daughter can't go back, and I can't go back either," Jon thought to himself. However, at that moment, his primary concern was whether the girl would be even more frightened. He observed her tightly grasping her mother's hand as if fearing her mother would vanish at any second.

"Don't worry, we'll find a way to get you back," Jon said. Although he mentioned "we", he was alone this time, without any colleagues accompanying him. He looked around. Despite Palm County being charming with its beautiful scenery and simple folk customs, the three strange things that had happened one after another were also ridiculous. He decided to go to the police station to find out what was going on.

After calming the mother and daughter here to rest, Jon drove to the police station.

## 5. Where to Go?

Julia felt as if time had stood still. It had been half a month since her last menstrual period when they arrived in Palm County, but now they had been here for a month and neither she nor her mother had experienced menstruation.

They had been trying various methods to leave Palm County throughout the month. Unfortunately, there were only two options for public transportation out of here: taking a train or car. They attempted to take a taxi, but no one was willing to pick them up because the drivers only operated within the city. In desperation, her mother tried calling her father in their hometown, but the county's electricity lines were down, causing communication issues both internally and externally.

This situation left them both desperate. Fortunately, the people in the county were extremely friendly and kind-hearted.

During their stay, they didn't need to spend any money at all. They were even receiving substantial pensions. The local police and the hotel owner were afraid that they would feel bored and restless so they frequently invited the mother and the daughter to watch various stage performances and participate in local folk activities.

Precisely because of this friendliness, the mother and daughter's fears were gradually dispelled.

By the second month, Julia always had the innocent smile on her face that a child should have, sweeping away the tension and melancholy she had when she first arrived. She enjoyed her life in Palm County and played with the local children. There were no homework assignments, no pressure to pursue higher education, and no competitions. She simply indulged in her hobbies without worrying about the outcomes.

Julia's mother also relished the genuine admiration she received from the locals. They praised her beauty and gentle and kind personality. In the previous city, few people had openly admired her so she had fallen in love with this place. She frequently visited the local orchards to help the fruit farmers pick fresh and delicious seasonal fruits. The farmers would thank her by offering various forms of compensation, such as cash, jewelry, or exquisite porcelain.

"Why don't you consider buying a house here?" an elderly fruit farmer suggested to Julia's mother. "The houses here are cheap and spacious, and the local policies are very favorable. If you buy a house the government will also be responsible for the decoration free of charge. They use the most environmentally friendly building materials and the latest designs."

"It's quite good," the mother said. "But we already have a house in our hometown, and our house is nice too. And the child's father..."

Speaking of this, the mother suddenly stopped.

"The child's father." She recalled the warm moments with her family, feeling a pang of sadness.

The carefree life of the past two months had made her forget that her family was far away, waiting for her to come back home.

"Oh my gosh!" The mother suddenly winced in pain, covering her face with her hands. It was the first time she cried since arriving in Palm County.

The fruit farmer on the sidelines hurriedly came forward and comforted her, saying. "It doesn't matter. We will find a way back soon. The government is doing everything it can to help you."

"No, no, no." The mother pushed away the kind-hearted auntie who tried to console her. "We, need to leave immediately. Right now. Let's go!"

After saying that, she stood up and quickly ran out of the orchard, heading towards the amusement park where a group of young girls were playing. She grabbed her daughter's hand and started walking away.

"Mom, what happened? Why are you in such a hurry?"

"We have to leave," the mother held her hand tightly without turning around. "We've forgotten our original purpose. We've been delayed here for too long. You still have homework to do. Have you forgotten it?"

"But Mom, I don't want to do homework anymore." The daughter suddenly broke free from her mother's grasp, causing the mother to stop and turn to look at her.

"Mom, I like it here," the daughter said with a smile on her face. This childlike innocence, reflected in her smile, hasn't been seen since she was in Grade 3 at the age of 9.

"I'm really happy here, Mom."

Looking at the daughter's hopeful expression on her face, the mother hugged her tightly.

"But don't you miss Dad?"

"Dad?"

The daughter muttered, unfamiliar with the term. She hadn't thought about him in a long time. She stayed quiet in her mother's embrace for a while, then looked up and said, "Mom, I still like here. Let's stay a little longer."

The mother smoothed her daughter's hair and nodded. "Alright, we'll stay for another week. Take this time to say goodbye to your friends."

## 6. Time Stood Still

Soon, Jon forgot that he was a journalist because he found the thing he loved most here, namely, pottery. He spent all day at the pottery house learning from the masters and creating his pottery works. Eventually, he became a famous pottery master in the county and held his first exhibition. Endless visits, and the admiration and encouragement he received made him feel a sense of honor. He even felt that creating pottery was his mission in life. As long as he dedicated himself to passion and hard work, he believed he could surpass most people. He couldn't believe what he had been doing before. It wasn't until he was over 40 years old that he entered the world of pottery. He tried to remember his previous job. What was his previous job?

Jon suddenly couldn't remember. One morning, while looking at himself in the mirror, he suddenly questioned his past. It seemed like his memories had vanished, and he could only recall his identity after coming to the county.

Time seemed to stand still. Jon touched his sideburns. It had been half a year since he came to Palm County. Over the past six months, his beard hadn't grown anymore, and his face hadn't changed in any way. It dawned on him that he used to be a journalist, a provincial journalist sent to investigate the disappearance of buildings.

"Ah!" He screamed as if he had just woken up from a dream. "It's been half a year!"

Half a year had gone by in the blink of an eye. The missing train station had never reappeared, and no one from the outside world had come again.

He suddenly remembered that there was a mother and daughter who had arrived in Palm County at the same time as him. He wondered how they were now.

Worry crept into his mind as he thought about the melancholic eyes of the girl and the fragile appearance of her mother. But  he reassured himself that the county was such a gentle and friendly place that they must have been treated well.

"It's none of my business. Maybe they have gone back already."

Thinking about this, he felt something wrong again.

"Shouldn't I go back too? What did my previous life look like?"

A series of questions came to Jon's mind. He held his head with his hands, feeling his mind go blank. He desperately shook his head, hoping to shake out the disappeared information.

Suddenly, a roar echoed through the sky. Jon rushed to the French window of his house, a gift from the county government recognizing his pottery skills. He happily stayed up all night while receiving the gift.

Peering outside, he saw nothing but the clear blue sky.

"Did I just mishear?"

At this point, there was another roar, and a dark shadow drifted through the sky.

This scene seemed familiar.

Jon felt unease and confusion envelop him. He ran to the door, changed his shoes, and pushed out the door.

### 7. Julia's Monologue

When I was a kid, I used to love dolls. Every birthday, my dad would buy me a new doll. When I was in my early childhood, it was just a small stuffed bunny or something like that. When I grew a little older it came to be a soft rag doll that looked like me, with big eyes and a round face. As I got older and older my parents started buying me dolls that could sing electronically. So from a young age, I learned how to talk to dolls. I was lonely and didn't have any siblings. Those dolls became my best friends. I loved taking care of them, dressing them up, feeding them, and even sleeping with them. I could spend the whole day just focusing on playing with and taming those dolls.

Then it seemed like I had a bit of ADHD, so my mom sent me to learn dance. It was a whole new world for me. At first, I thought dancing was just so beautiful. The initial reason was quite simple. One day, I saw a dancer walking around my school in a beautiful red dance costume and I was mesmerized by the beauty of it. That's when my mom decided to send me to dance school. But once I started learning dance, I realized it wasn't as glamorous and romantic as I had imagined. The process of learning dance was painful, especially the repetition of basic skills. I had to slowly memorize each movement step-by-step. It wasn't just about getting the movements right; I also had to focus on my breathing and posture. It was nothing like what I had pictured in my mind.

Many times, I wanted to give up, but my mom wouldn't hear of it. She told me that perseverance was an essential trait for success in life. At that time, I didn't fully understand what perseverance meant, but my mom would be there with me during practice sessions. When I was doing leg flexibility exercises, she watched me; when I was bending down, she ate ice cream; when I was crying, she waited here silently. This kind of companionship made me stick slowly. It wasn't until I won first prize in a county dance competition that I realized the true meaning of learning dance. It was about making incremental progress every single day. The hardships and sweat during the process ultimately forged glory and brilliance. Ever since then, I stopped complaining. Every time I practiced, I felt a sense of calm. When my legs ached, I knew it meant progress. The pain was a sign of progress.

In the same way, I fell in love with many things later. I developed a passion for mathematics and consistently took first place in exams. I discovered my love for running and even completed a full marathon in five hours. All of these achievements were made possible through the work ethic instilled in me by my mother. Giving up was never an option for me.

And I understand that some of the things you have experienced in your life, whether good or bad, will always turn over. Pain, tears, glory, and success are all temporary; the suffering and joys of others today will someday come to you as well. This feeling keeps me calm amidst the volatility of life. I believe a life without emotional ups and downs is not a complete life.

Even though I'm only in my teens I feel like I've grasped some principles of life. Life is about going with the flow while trying to guide its course. A good steersman doesn't rigidly stick to their actions, nor do they completely surrender to the ebbs and flows of life.

Self-will and natural will are intertwined friends, supporting and harmonizing with each other.

Julia, written after being in Palm County for 6 months.

## 8. Fortress in Palm County

The wind is gradually blowing, the dark clouds gathering and the sky growing darker.

Jon walked along the road noticing that there were fewer and fewer pedestrians around. He seemed to have lost his way. Despite spending six months in Palm County, he had explored almost every corner except the place right in front of him. The surrounding buildings had a unique design, with a powerful aura despite their gray and earthy appearance.

This scene piqued his curiosity. As he continued on his way, a few large, dark birds suddenly appeared in the sky, emitting harsh cries from time to time.

They must be crows, Jon thought.

The dark clouds above grew thicker, and the wind grew stronger. Jon pressed on against the wind. All of a sudden he encountered a cliff in front of him. The ground abruptly dropped off. His heart leaped into his throat, and his legs went numb. Looking down from the edge of the cliff he could see the entire town below. Thankfully, the drop wasn't too high. Street houses were lined up like terraces, creating a warm and beautiful scene.

Jon took a few steps back and looked around. The dark sky seemed almost within reach. The big black birds, who screamed terribly, gathered more and more under the dark clouds. The roads, both above and below the cliffs, twisted and turned. A sense of sadness crept into his heart inexplicably leaving him wondering why he'd suddenly developed such emotions.

I must have reached a mountaintop, surrounded by scattered houses and a monumental structure resembling a memorial.

Jon stepped closer to the monumental structure and discovered it was a tower-shaped fortress. He walked around, only to find a hidden underground passage. Looking down, the dark inside seemed to swallow up everything. He felt a tingling sensation in his spine. However, the strong curiosity still pushed him forward into the black passageway.

He took out his phone from his pocket, maximizing the flashlight's brightness, and walked along the right wall of the underground passage.

It's dark and a little cold inside, but there's no smell of dust or decay. This couldn't be a place where nobody had been before. He continued to move forward, and his field of vision gradually widened, and he also saw vaguely some objects such as vases, tables, and chairs.

"Someone must clean this place regularly," Jon surmised.

There was still a path ahead. Jon kept walking as more and more calligraphy, paintings, and other ceramic utensils and objects appeared around. He noticed a small circular clearing ahead. The ground was arranged in a row with regularly arranged symbols and characters. It looked like Chinese, but it was also a bit like Oracle (bone script).

Jon opened the translation app on his phone and input text and photos on the wall into engine search. It turned out to be the language of the Palm people, an ancient language. Jon proceeded to input another piece of text on the wall into the translation engine. It turned out to be a poem:

*People should be artworks, not just artists.*
*Carve yourself, instead of burning away in a blaze;*
*Nourish yourself, not drain yourself dry;*
*Forgive yourself, as it sets others free;*
*Embrace yourself, and you'll embrace the world.*
*Both mind and body need exercise, through reading and doing*
*sports.*

He inputted the other pieces of text on the wall into the translation engine:

*To win, to accept failure; To be brave, to confront weakness;*

*Learn to neglect results and value the process;*

*Choose what's important, and let the rest disband.*

*I wrote this in the hope that 500 years from now, I will be able to find myself and witness the lingering fragrance of a woman's soul from five centuries ago. There are countless opportunities for me to discover my true self by following the footsteps of profound literature and philosophy. This is the sacred mission of being a disseminator of thoughts.*

- Queen Jacqueline

"Who's the Queen Jacqueline?" Jon looked at the final signature and couldn't help but wonder, "These are profound principles of doing things and being a person. They are very empowering, but I have no clue who left them behind."

Jon turned around and glanced down, fixating on the outer boundary of the eight-diagram circle, just a meter away from his toes, and came to a halt.

"Should I step into this eight-diagram tactic?" Jon was stuck in the same spot, contemplating his options.

Suddenly, he felt a suffocating sensation as if the air around him no longer circulated. Then came dizziness and the whole world spinning.She staggered, and her phone accidentally fell to the ground, shining onto the ceiling, and revealing a huge painting. Just as she was astonished, everything went black before her eyes, and Jane fainted.

## 9. A Marriage of Collective Gain

Jacqueline's fiancé is the son of her father's comrade. Her parents are highly satisfied with this prospective son-in-law, and they have no aversion towards him either. Despite his physical appearance, being overweight with a small mustache under his nose, he is kind and friendly. Additionally, Jacqueline has a high status in Palm Country with a distinguished family background.

"So many girls dream of marrying such a family. You should cherish it," Jacqueline's brother said to her.

She has an older brother and a younger brother. They have all been very nice to Jacqueline. Since childhood, she has received the best education resources, the most attention for growth, and the most affection from her family.

Therefore, the day Jacqueline got married became the biggest joy in Palm Country. People lined the streets to celebrate, and all the stars and influential figures in the county came to attend the wedding. Everyone praised and blessed this perfect union.

Seeing her parents, brothers, and the people of her country looking so happy, Jacqueline was also very happy inexplicably.

There were no major ups and downs in the days after the marriage. Since marrying her current husband, the business scale of her family has gradually expanded. Her older brother has taken charge of the dominant company. Her younger brother was transferred to the central region for development with the coordination of resources from her husband. Her parents have moved to a bigger house. It seems that everyone's lives have significantly improved and enhanced. However, Jacqueline often finds herself feeling somewhat empty. She can't say whether she loves her husband or has any other feelings. Sometimes she wonders what Romance is. Perhaps she has never truly experienced it before and was simply placed on the "best path". After getting married, her former classmates and friends came to congratulate her, saying that she looked more beautiful and even younger than before.

Indeed, she not only becomes younger but also becomes richer. Thanks to her marriage, her father's status in the country is equivalent to the country governor.

This is a marriage that benefits everyone.

In the dead of night, Jacqueline often stayed awake all night. Is it beneficial for everyone? Really?

After countless sleepless nights pondering over it, she finally asked herself: Am I benefiting from this?

During the silent nights, she looked at her husband who was asleep. She couldn't help but think of him as a pig. He was simple-minded, amiable, ate voraciously, and rarely had any deep thoughts. How did I fall in love with him?

Hold on, do I love him?

What is love?

What is romance?

She looked at her husband sleeping peacefully, a simple man who probably never grappled with such questioning.

But this is the person I get along with every day!

She turned away, not wanting to see the face of that pig. A tear rolled down Jacqueline's cheek and landed on the pillow.

"How can I love someone like this? It's simply impossible!"

When she found the answer, tears streamed down her face. In this marriage where everyone benefited, she was the only one sacrificing herself.

"Although I am surrounded by endless love, I am just a pet without self-will, a delicate Persian cat, an exquisite vase, the brightest jewel in the crown, forever basking in the shelter and radiance of the outside world."

Her tears grew more intense, and the pillow gradually became soaked. Once the soul awakened, it was hard to calm down.

Therefore, the next morning, she fled Palm Country, leaving only a note expressing her desire to find freedom and true love.

Jacqueline's family was in distress, especially her mother. Jacqueline had always been obedient, and her sudden departure made the mother fall ill.

At this point, war broke out. Jacqueline's brothers, husband, and father, as central figures in Palm Country, were all involved in the war.

The war was fierce. The enemy possessed dozens of times of military strength and firepower than that of Palm Country. Soon, corpses littered the streets. The ruthless enemy not only attacked the peace-loving country but showed no mercy to the ordinary citizens. After three months of occupation, the opposing army massacred the entire country.

They piled the corpses onto a fortress, but as the corpses decomposed, the putrid smell attracted hordes of crows and vultures. Hence, the enemy set the corpses ablaze for three days and nights, burning everything to ashes. During the burning process, the flames crackled and emitted desperate cries, as if the screams and struggles of thousands of dead people.

## 10. When Are We Going Home?

Julia had been enjoying her time in Palm County for the past six months. She didn't have to worry about school or deal with complicated relationships with classmates. It was a period of unprecedented freedom for her. However, over these six months, her body hadn't grown or developed, which greatly worried her mother.

The mother had always wanted to bring Julia back home, but Julia insisted on staying for an additional six months. During this time, Julia not only experienced physical freedom, but also enjoyed the freedom to dance, run wild in the mountains, and engage in unrestricted conversations with anyone in the city.

She enjoyed absolute spiritual freedom. Everyone here encouraged and supported her to do anything, making her feel like a revered princess. She had been treated like a princess at home by her parents, grandparents, and maternal grandparents. They indulged her in her unreasonable tantrums. However, both her paternal and maternal grandparents passed away at an early age. After their passing, her parents became occupied with their business, and they rarely spent time with her like they used to do when she was younger. In Palm County, more people loved and accepted her, making her feel like she was back in those days filled with love and attention. This makes her reluctant to part ways and even wants to bring her father here.

"Are you awake, my little piggy?" With a knock on the door and her mother's gentle call, Julia reluctantly sat up in bed, still half-asleep, and looked at her mother who entered the room and said, "Hurry up and get ready. Today, we're going home!"

"Mom, really?"

"What do you mean, really?"

"You promised to bring Dad here, and once we see him, we'll be back."

"Yes. Hurry up! Wash your face and brush your teeth."

Upon hearing these words, Julia jumped off the bed.

Today was in poor weather conditions. With rare dark clouds gathering overhead, it looked like rain today. Julia and her mother walked on the road and didn't bring many things. Julia observed her mother's face, her lips tightly closed, walking forward with determination. It seemed that her mother made up her mind to take Julia out of Palm County this time, but she didn't know what kind of plan her mother had in mind.

Over the past six months, the mother had tried various methods to leave.

The train station disappeared, so they went to the bus station. But the bus station was also gone, so they tried to take a taxi. However, none of the taxi drivers were willing to take them away; they only accepted fares within the city. Although Julia enjoyed these days, her mother felt hopeless. Her mother believed that it wasn't their home even though Palm County was good. Free, bright, and abundant in material resources. The mother continues to hold fond memories of Julia's father and other relatives. Even though the hometown she came from is not perfect, its people possess a tough and untamed character. Nevertheless, it is undeniably her hometown!

For the past six months, the mother has been trying to establish contact with the outside world. However, it seemed that there was no connection with the outside world here. She never saw anyone come into the county from outside. In times of despair, the mother suddenly remembered Jon, the one who came here together with them. She didn't know how Jon had been doing for the past six months. She found Jon's number in the phone book and had an appointment with him at Fountain Square on the western side of Palm County.

By now, the mother had already taken the daughter to Fountain Square. Replaced by a fortress, the fountain is now nothing more than a memory. Hovering above, dozens of crows darken the sky, sending shivers down the spines of both the mother and Julia.

"Mom, let's go back. I'm scared," Julia trembled as she held her mother's hand.

"Don't be afraid. Mom is here!"

The mother held Julia's hand. Once upon a time, the mother was also a little girl scared of everything, but since Julia was born and her mother passed away, she became the "mother" who could bear everything. She couldn't be afraid at any time, especially in front of her daughter.

The mother held the daughter's hand and circled the fortress until she spotted a hole leading underground. She wondered if they should go down and explore. Perhaps the secret to leaving Palm County lay within this passage.

Just as the mother hesitated, Julia had already walked towards the underground passage.

"Sweetheart, come back!" the mother shouted in horror.

The daughter turned back, looked at her mother, and said, "Mom, I know what you're thinking. Let's go down and take a look. We must go home this time."

The mother looked at the daughter and noticed a newfound maturity and sensibility in her young face. This further strengthened her determination to go home. She wanted her daughter to live a normal life, even if it meant facing challenges and uncertainties along the way. It was an essential part of growing up for a girl. No matter how many hardships were outside, she would accompany her daughter through them. But she couldn't stay here and stop growing.

Thinking of this, tears welled up in the mother's eyes. She walked in front of the daughter and pulled her behind.

"Stay behind me."

## 11. The Second Massacre

Ten years later, Jacqueline has become the queen of a small to Medium country in the East. She not only commanded her army but also had a new husband and children.

When Jacqueline returned to Palm Country, she found that the buildings, her family, and the people she once knew were all gone. The country had been renamed to Saiya. From the local people, she learned that her hometown had been massacred ten years ago after she left home. Upon hearing this news, Jacqueline was filled with grief and anger. She coughed up blood in agony, feeling guilty for her past recklessness, regretful for not fulfilling her responsibilities towards her family, and burning with rage at the cruelty of the enemy.

She then gathered the army she had established in the Medium country and launched an attack against Palm.

Queen Jacqueline's army was brave and skilled in battle. They were all young individuals who possessed strength, intelligence, and bravery. Thus, they swiftly captured the king and army of the country of Saiya. Similarly, Queen Jacqueline chose to massacre the city. Some of the people were buried alive under the castle, while others were burned inside it.

After the second massacre, Queen Jacqueline found her former house and the fortress where the corpses were burned. She reconstructed the fortress and engraved the names of all the people of Palm Country who had once resided there.

After the fortress was rebuilt, it appeared as if nothing had happened. However, above the fortress in the sky, people could always see groups of crows circling, eagerly searching for something.

Queen Jacqueline ruled the Medium country and designated Palm Country as its dependent state, renaming it Palm County. Due to deep nostalgia for her hometown and deceased loved ones, she empowered Palm County with the best economic and political policies. The finest resources were imported to Palm County, as well as the best social welfare policies. Only the most talented and morally upright individuals from a Medium country could obtain citizenship in Palm County.

At that moment, Jon suddenly opened his eyes. He looked at the surroundings, drenched in cold sweat from the scene of the massacre in his dream. As he looked around, a stench of decay filled the air. Yes, it was the odor of decay. Could this be the fortress that was burned during the city massacre? Was the dream he just had a historical narrative of the development of Palm County, is it a country previously? And were the words engraved on the monument he saw upon arriving at the fortress the names of thousands of people from Palm County? Nope. The people of disappeared Palm Country!

The cold wind howled outside the fortress. It seems like a resentful cry, intending to tear the entire world into pieces. Jon was deeply touched by this scene. Memories of the horrifying scenes of massacred people in his dream flooded back, and Jon felt an acute pain in his heart. He put his hand to the heart and began to weep.

Suddenly, he felt a burst of light in front of him. He looked up and saw a woman dressed in white standing in front of him. Looking closely, he felt so familiar. He took a closer look and recalled where he had seen this woman before. A realization struck him abruptly. This was exactly the Queen Jacqueline appeared in his dream.

It was indeed Queen Jacqueline in his dream!

He couldn't help but be astonished, unable to distinguish whether he was awake or still trapped in a dream.

Right now, the woman in white in front of him was smiling.

## 12. The Mother's Monologue

As they enter middle age, many women become powerful. They are financially stable, possess strong capabilities, and radiate beauty. They can have as many children as they want. For most people, reaching middle age brings an expected scenario with multiple children and a husband who is only bound by family ties or the unfortunate reality of a broken marriage.

But in my concept, what's the use of having so much money if there is no love, warmth, and understanding from your other half? Isn't it boring to have a child and raise him or her alone? The purpose of life is to perceive and appreciate various relationships and intertwine within them.

Those Buddhist practitioners have told me how wonderful and detached they are. In my view, I should have been aware of the hardships in the world before I was born. Life is always painful.

That's why I chose to immerse myself in the bustling world. A joyful life should be light, just like a soul not attached to the physical body, existing like a stream of consciousness in the air.

It seems that all choices in life come with a cost. All beings suffer, and no one can mock others.

Therefore, my daughter is like my second life. I love her more than myself. She is my work, the bright outlet in my painful and boring life.

Looking back, my life has had its ups and downs. I no longer experience intense emotional fluctuations over many things as I did when I was young. I once told myself: if one day I know I have to win, I will firmly move forward without sadness or impatience; if one day I know I will lose, I will still firmly move forward because the result has already been determined.

In the past, I always yearned for victory. My blood would boil when participated in a game, but that sentiment has faded considerably. Through experience, I have come to understand that every individual in society, regardless of whether they are perceived as good or bad, faces their unique challenges. They possess their logical frameworks. No matter how bad they may seem to others, they believe they are right. Instead of criticizing, I prefer to embrace humanity.

The incessant sound of cicadas fills the air. Nobody knows where they hide. As soon as the heat wave arrives, they start roaring madly. For cicadas, their purpose in life is to sing throughout the summer and then die, much like a microcosm of human existence. People clamor and expend their energy during the most fervent years of their lives, but as the autumn breeze sets in, their voices grow increasingly subdued, until their lives are extinguished.

Life is an experience. What others envy may not be suitable for me, and what others despise may not make me feel sad. Pitiful humans seek meaning and a sense of existence from God, but these things are ultimately swept away like the Turkish carpet and more likely to be trampled on. That is why the Dao De Jing states that water is adept at nourishing all things without contending with them, lingering in places that are disliked by everyone. Therefore, it is closest to the "Dao".

My daughter seems to have a special connection with the number 3. She was born on March 3, 1992, at 6:10 p.m. She prefers to incorporate the singular numbers 3, 6, and 9 into her actions. She is particularly sensitive to trajectory and always insists on turning right if she accidentally turns left. She likes to draw trajectories in her notebook, claiming she wants to predict my fortune.

Every time she does this, I don't know whether to laugh or cry.

She is highly intelligent and rarely forgets what she hears. Additionally, she excels at memorizing plot-related things. I believe her talents are best suited for trading stocks: drawing charts and creating stories, or writing as well. Consequently, I place great importance on her education and fostering her strengths.

The daughter is caring and loves me. At most of the time, she is stubborn and has her own opinions. No one can subdue her, and she always enjoys arguing with her father. She is quite talkative.

I cherish every moment spent with my daughter, never averting my eyes from her. Sometimes, even when hungry, I find myself pondering what kind of person she will marry in the future. In the past, I always anticipated that she would marry true love, marry the person she loves the most, and marry Mr. Perfect at first sight. Right now, my hopes remain the same.

Why? Because I know that loving someone is more fulfilling than being loved. I hope that my daughter can continuously create her happiness and to be innovative in her pursuits. I hope she becomes a sun, a star, shining and radiating on her own, rather than relying on the light of others.

Dear sweetheart, I cannot accompany you throughout your entire life. An enduring companion is paramount. I hope you will have a warm and harmonious family in the future. Do not dedicate your life entirely to any single pursuit, but rather become a completely ordinary person. Live your life with peace of mind, diligently fulfill your responsibilities, and embrace the full breadth of life's experiences. If you are fortunate, you can stand a little higher. That would be great.

All in all, my Sweetheart, I hope you be a complete and powerful individual. And we, people who love you, will always be with you, protect you, and appreciate your radiance.

- Mom

## 13. Gathering

What the hell is going on? The grand wedding, the war, the slaughter, the fortress… Are these real? Jon's mind was in turmoil, and he was about to ask when the woman in white spoke up.

"Yeah, everything in your dreams happened."

Jon was astonished, trembling as he looked at the woman in white with disbelief.

"Are you Jacqueline? The queen who returned after running away from home and implemented the massacre?"

"Yes, that's me," Jacqueline replied, with a mysterious smile on her lips. "But all of this happened 999 years ago."

Jon swallowed hard, unable to speak due to the tremendous shock.

"You must have a lot of questions in your mind right now. Why am I still here after a thousand years? Which part of the dream was true? And what happened to the buildings that disappeared in Palm County?"

Though he hadn't said a word, it seemed as if Jacqueline could see into his soul. Jon pinched his thigh hard. The real pain made him realize that everything in front of him wasn't fake. He quickly got up and prayed to the woman in white.

"So, you must be the ancestor of Palm County. You are the queen often mentioned by the people. It was you who founded the entire city."

Jacqueline looked at Jon, who was bowing down and praying. A satisfied smile appeared on her face.

"Yes, I'm the one who founded the entire county. That queen Jacqueline in people's mouths. A long time ago, there weren't many people here yet. This county town is located on a transit border. Once upon a time, it was a small, independent state. My father and husband were almost like kings. Everything that happened here later was just like in your dreams."

"But why did you flee from Palm County? No, I mean Palm Country. And why did you come back?"

Jacqueline looked at Jon and smiled as if she had anticipated that he would ask this question.

"This is a question that has perplexed people for thousands of years. Every newcomer will ask this question."

"Every newcomer?"

"Yes, in fact, most of the people in Palm County, the vast majority, are outsiders. The group of people who once built a new homeland here were my troops. They have already passed away. If it weren't for the descendants of those few people, Palm County would have disappeared long ago."

"Are they all outsiders like me?"

"Let me answer your first question now. Be patient, and I'll answer all of your questions one by one. Please don't lie on the ground. Come and sit at the table over here. We'll have new guests soon."

"New guests?"

Just then, a shrill scream echoed in his ears. Jon turned his head and found that it was the little girl he met half a year ago, Julia. She was looking at the shining woman in white, letting out a terrified scream. Her mother was standing next to her. It seemed that they had also dreamed about everything Jon had just experienced before entering the underground fortress.

"Are you... are you the Queen Jacqueline?" the girl asked in horror, then looked at Jon.    "Are you the uncle who will lead us out?"

## 14. The Queen's Narration

"Many people have asked me why I remain unsatisfied with such a privileged life and a wonderful family. They wonder if my departure from Palm Country was due to foreseeing the events that would unfold here. My answer is 'No.' I did not know what would happen here. I left the country and my beloved family simply because I had never experienced the intense and profound feeling of love. I'm not talking about the feelings of others towards me, but my feelings towards others. It's not just about humans; I had never truly experienced what it means to have a deep passion or love even when it comes to things or certain pursuits."

Before leaving Palm Country, I had an almost perfect life. My father cherished me like a bright pearl in the palm. My brothers were willing to sacrifice their lives to protect me. My mother was my closest confidante. My husband was loyal and deeply loved me. I had the most precious treasure in the world, the most perfect friendships, the most loyal companions, and the gentlest care. I had it all. I felt like a carrier of love and glory. Even if looking through historical books, few princesses have had such a life."

As she told us this, Jacqueline paused, and the three people sitting across the table from her were captivated by her words.

"It's ridiculous. I left because I had never experienced pain. Many people find this hard to believe. How can anyone willingly seek out pain? But there is a kind of pain that one cannot experience unless they go through it. It's called the absence of pain. Without pain, there is no joy. Without intense pain, one cannot experience true happiness. I believe my parents, brothers, and husband have all experienced this. They have endured hardships, ups and downs, and sufferings to protect me. They have found happiness, while I have always had to bear this heavy burden of "Love". It has prevented me from truly understanding love. I no longer comprehend what love is, and I've even started to resent my husband, believing that marrying him was the root of all my troubles."

Jacqueline glanced at the mother. The mother pursed her lips, seemingly having experienced a similar situation before coming to the county. She had a big quarrel with her husband (Julia's father) before bringing Julia to the competition.

Jacqueline continued, "So, I ran away from my husband and came to the capital of a Medium country. There, nobody knew whether I was a princess or a queen. They treated me like an ordinary person. I received education, worked, and built my team there. Gradually, I gained fame in a Medium country and accumulated considerable wealth through my skills. All of this made me genuinely happy because it relied on my abilities, not just on the support of my parents, brothers, or husband.

Just when I returned to my hometown, hoping to share these moments with my family, I discovered that everything in my hometown had vanished. The savage Palm army massacred everyone, including my parents and brothers. Anger fueled my hatred, so, like a man, I led the army, defeated Palm's army, and wiped out their entire population. Right here, in the very fortress where we stand, fires burned again and again, devouring my people and their people."

Upon hearing this, the three modern people at the table looked at each other in astonishment. The woman in white in front of them wasn't just the graceful and generous goddess of Palm County, but also the determined Empress Jacqueline. She could be as gentle as water, as resolute as steel, and as fierce as a warrior to lead her troops into battle.

A sense of solemn respect permeated throughout the entire fortress.

"After the war, I rebuilt Palm County. I brought the team and army I had conquered from the Medium country, made Palm County a dependent country, and transformed my former nation into a nice county to live and work in. I introduced the best resources and policies of the Medium country in Palm County and drafted a separate governance plan for this small county."

## 15. The Queen's 21 Maxims

1. Where there is a soul, there is brightness.

2. Life is a game. Only by complying with the rules can one have the chance to showcase oneself.

3. Action and process are both the consequences and rewards in themselves.

4. Change should be driven by an intrinsic sense of shame, rather than someone else 's morality.

5. Everyone gets old. The strong should know how to give space to the weak.

6. Rationality should not be pitted against emotion.

7. With love in your heart, you will be tolerant of everything.

8. No one can monopolize the brilliance of God; people should mutually respect each other.

9. Hope built on bubbles holds no value.

10. Even if the sunshine doesn't fall upon you, it will shine upon others; it's better to actively pursue the sunshine.

11. Should one break the mirror just for his ugly appearance?

12. In the absence of things we enjoy, all that remains is vanity and ostentation.

13. The masses possess a vision akin to that of blind individuals.

14. With a rooted mind, one's journey in life will not be swayed by the current; with a mindful stride, one can select their path amidst the multitude of possibilities.

15. Don't die with those who are already gone; instead, live well with those who are alive.

16. Once capable of altering destiny, one should radiate their light.

17. Love yourself like the person who loves you

18. Possessions do not belong solely to me but exist for my use.

19. Only when you completely let go of the external world can you fully obey your true self.

20. Most women desire marriage and children not because it's inherent to their nature, but a worldly task and a sense of responsibility based on love.

21. Happiness is a fusion of joy and pain. Some simplify happiness to only joy, but that is one-sided. Because where there is joy, there will inevitably be pain, just like night and day. Without night, there would be no day. The extent of happiness depends on one's ability to master joy and pain, as they are both unavoidable in life. Hence, it is crucial to exert control over one's joy and pain.

## 16. Jacqueline's Horses

The year I came to the mid-sized country, I was just 23 years old. That same year, I started looking for a job and successfully got a position in a horse stable, handling the financial work. Recognizing my intelligence and enthusiasm for learning, the boss swiftly delegated to me the responsibility of overseeing all financial matters at the stable. Within less than a year, I became proficient in the intricacies of managing a horse stable.

At the age of 24, I embarked on an entrepreneurial journey with a few colleagues and established our small-scale horse stable.

At the age of 25, I had accumulated a small fortune due to the successful operation of the horse stable. To further expand my knowledge and experience, I went to two Large countries.

At the age of 27, I expanded the scale of my horse stable and set up branch offices in large countries.

At the age of 28, I extended the industry chain of the horse stable to finance, providing horse leasing services. This led me to enter into a business partnership with the military, and it was during this time that I met my second husband.

At the age of 29, a significant number of my horses were requisitioned by the military due to the ongoing conflict. As a result, my reputation within the military began to flourish.

At the age of 30, I had virtually assembled my army. All matters related to the horse business should be directed to me.

At the age of 31, I extended the horse business to technologies, providing more advanced and sophisticated horses and transportation tools.

At the age of 32, many financially struggling horse farms, even small-scale countries, have submitted to me, hoping for my acquisition and financial assistance.

At the age of 33, this Medium country bestowed upon me the highest honor. I possessed the corresponding military authority and fiscal powers.

At the age of 34, I returned home with all these achievements, only to find that the horses I had once raised had crushed my homeland.

Everything that followed was as you dreamed.

The three major industrial chains in this medium-sized country were horses, finance, and technologies. Besides, the cultural and artistic industries were highly developed. Over the past decade in business, I have strategically established the core lifelines of these industries.

"Then what's the deal with the disappeared train station? What's going on with the communication facilities here? And your people, although very nice, seem quite different from people outside," Jon asked.

"The station didn't disappear because it never existed." Jacqueline wore a mysterious smile as she replied,

"The people who can come here are carefully selected by us through big data analysis."

She waved her hand, revealing hundreds of IT professionals wearing Bluetooth headsets and operating computers behind the transparent glass screens.

"The IT technology in Palm County is second to none. We have deliberately maintained a primitive way of life externally to preserve the quality of life for our people amidst the advancement of communication. Our fruits and vegetables are the freshest in the world. Our water is the purest and sweetest. Our people - every individual you encounter in Palm County, possess hidden talents and skills that are beyond what meets the eye."

The three of them were amazed as they gazed upon the hundreds of IT professionals engrossed in their work and the data displayed on the large screen.

"But why did you choose us to come here? We don't possess any extraordinary skills. We're just ordinary people. All we want is to go back, right now. We have our own lives and don't want to be trapped in a small town like this for the rest of our lives," the young mother said, tears streaming down her face. "Everyone has the right to choose their own life, and staying here is not what we are eager for!"

Witnessing her mother in tears, Julia quickly approached to offer comfort.

"Yeah, why choose us?" Jon also asked, " Why were we selected among so many people?"

## 17. Strong Vitality

Queen Jacqueline turned and walked towards the glass door, pressing a button. The enormous glass screen immediately transformed into a wall, making the bustling staff disappear from her sight. She pressed another button next to the door, and the wall transformed into the train station.

The station was bustling with people coming and going, creating a lively scene.

"Every newcomer to Palm County will go through the same experiences you have had, and every citizen has the right to choose whether to leave or stay. This is the freedom granted to you by the guardians of this county."

"That's great! So, when can we leave?" the mother asked.

"At any time. I can send you away today. But once you leave here, all memories about this place will be removed from your mind.

You will forget everything here and return to your previous life."

Upon hearing this, Julia hesitated, and her mother was also in doubt.

"But why did you choose us?" Jon asked. "I mean, why we were chosen to be sample citizens since you have so many selections in your database?"

"I am not Jacqueline. I am just a successor," stated the woman in white. "But you can call me Jacqueline. All of her successors are called Jacqueline. I am the one who has been selected as the most suitable successor from among numerous clones."

"I chose you because you are exceptionally pure, kind, full of love, and talented. In our extensive database, we have collected information and experiences from all individuals, enabling us to analyze their personalities and genetic indices. Based on these analyses, you were selected."

The three people seated around the table grew restless. A feeling of apprehension, stemming from being under surveillance, sent shivers down their spines. Just as Jon was about to speak, Jacqueline preempted him.

"You must be wondering how we obtained this data, whether such manipulation is ethical, and if we violated your rights?"

Jacqueline cast a sweeping glance at the crowd before fixing her gaze on her mother.

"You have always desired to escape from this marriage. Due to the consideration of the child and the parents, you have been unable to leave your husband. You love your husband and continue to serve him wholeheartedly, despite the personality differences. Now, we are allowing you to make a fresh choice."

Her gaze then shifted to Julia.

"You detest endless assignments and homework, but you love dancing. According to the Eight Diagrams in *The Book of Changes*, 'The overbearing dragon is repentant.' We awarded you the second prize because we believed in the principle of things turning in the opposite direction when reaching an extreme. We are concerned that you might become arrogant if given the first prize. We fear that you may not be able to handle the repercussions that come with the glory of being a champion. We hope that you can always strive for improvement and maintain self-discipline."

Jacqueline finally focused her gaze on him and said,

"Haven't you achieved everything you desired here? Your ideal and desired life of ease?"

The three of them looked at each other, unsure of what to say.

Jacqueline continued, "Now I give you a chance to make a new choice. Of course, you can return to your previous lives, but think carefully: Is what you want a compromise with reality? A cowardice based on stability? Or a careful consideration for your future and the future of your descendants? **You are certainly free to choose to go back or come forward. You can even choose any place in the world, as long as you are not hindered by fear,**

**restricted by loved ones, confined by tradition, or influenced by authority**."

These words deeply resonated with everyone present. The three of them looked at each other, pondering their options.

"You can make your choices now. If you choose to stay, you will be granted citizenship here and have the life you desire. If you choose to leave, our roc will send you back home, and you will still have the life you desire.

### 18. leave or stay?

With a smile on her face, Jacqueline looked at Julia, then at the mother, before fixing her gaze on Jon.

"I … I choose to stay," Jon said. "Palm County is like a land of idyllic beauty. I've read about the idyllic life of Utopia in textbooks since I was a child, but I never thought I would come to such a place in my lifetime. I believe this kind of life is a dream for millions of people, so I want to continue, to stay here and become a part of it, to serve you, my Queen."

Jacqueline nodded with a smile, then turned her gaze back to the mother. The mother looked at Jacqueline and the daughter once again. She came over and squatted in front of her daughter, gently asking her,

"Sweetheart, tell me, do you like dancing?"

The daughter looked at her mother but didn't respond.

"I mean, are you happy when you dance?"

"Well, not always, but most of the time."

"Are you willing to choose this path continuously? To keep striving and working hard for what you love?"

The daughter pondered, unsure of how to answer. She knew her mother wanted to go home.

"You don't have to worry about me," Mom seemed to perceive her thoughts. "I fully respect your choice. Throughout your upbringing, I have wholeheartedly supported whatever you are passionate about. I will use the best resources available to pave the way for you and will also accompany you on this journey."

Looking at her mother, Julia recalled her experiences since she was young. She remembered her lack of natural flexibility, her stiff back like a steel plate. Other kids could do splits, while she could barely get her legs to a 90-degree angle on the bar. Other kids could do front and back bridges, while she could only manage a slight bend. Dance wasn't suitable for her.

Julia remembered that she always excelled in mathematics and her essays were always chosen as exemplary readings by her teachers in her hometown. Everyone called her a talented girl. She reminisced about the honors she received in primary school and middle school, and how she struggled to conquer dance. Perhaps it was her indomitable spirit that pushed her to devote so much effort to dancing. Maybe it was because dance competitions allowed her to see a different world, from small towns to provincial capital cities, and even to the capital of the country, that she fell in love with dance. Ultimately, what she loved was the sense of honor and the colorful world it offered. With these thoughts in mind, Julia shook her head.

"Mom, I am not willing. Dancing is too painful and not suitable for me. I want to study and explore more places. Let's go home."

The mother looked at Julia seriously.

"Are you truly unwilling? I'm not deceiving you. If you like it, whatever you choose, I will accompany you."

"Mom, it's true. I don't want to dance forever. I want to study hard and surpass others." She was referring to a few academic competitors at school.

The mother embraced her daughter with great satisfaction, then turned to Jacqueline and said, "There's no need to be conflicted. Ever since Julia was born, I knew that my lifelong mission was to protect her. Whatever she desires, I will wholeheartedly provide for her and accompany her. That's my purpose in life. So, we decided to return to the previous place. Although it's not perfect there, full of dirty humanity and intense competition, my child needs to have a complete life, to truly engage with the crowd, just like your ancestors did, and win glory and respect for her 'crown'. So, even though the road ahead may be challenging, we must go back. That is the battlefield for my daughter and me."

Jacqueline's eyes were filled with pride as she looked at her mother with contentment and said,

"You are truly admirable. As you wish, I will send a roc to safely escort you back home."

After expressing their gratitude to Jacqueline individually, the screen on the wall suddenly changed and turned into an actual wall. Immediately, the wall split open from the middle, and a small car emerged through it. The driver was the auntie who frequently chatted with Julia's mother at the food market. After exchanging friendly greetings with the auntie, Julia and her mother got into the car and followed her. The auntie drove along the tunnel of the underground fortress, while Julia focused on the pitch-dark road ahead, with only the bright light from the car's headlights illuminating the surroundings. Everything was just like the day she arrived. It was silent, with only the sound of the car's engine. Sitting in the car with her mother, Julia felt as if they had been abandoned by the whole world. Looking around, she pondered that life might be like this: a beginning is also an ending, and an ending is also a new beginning. Therefore, parting and reunion should be regarded as ordinary occurrences in life.

"Later, you will board the 'roc', the boss's small private plane. Remember to follow the rules." said the auntie who was driving.

"What rules?" Julia asked.

"Do not look backward when flying forward, and do not look downward when flying upward. Or, everything may become futile."

"Okay." Both the mother and daughter responded.

The auntie glanced at Julia in the rear-view mirror and revealed a smile.

**Do not look downward when Running forward, and do not look downward when flying upward.** Reciting these two sentences in mind, the mother and daughter returned to their hometown under the escort of the "roc". Although they stayed in Palm County for half a year, for their hometown, only 6 days had passed. Everything remained the same, and everyone believed that Julia and her mother were just on a normal business trip.

Strangely enough, contrary to what Jacqueline said, the mother and daughter did not forget about this experience. Many years later, Julia often wondered if she had been to a place called Palm County, a small town the size of a palm, where there were kind and friendly people, picturesque scenery, and fragrant and sweet fruits. The women there had no pressure. They only pursued beauty for themselves and danced for the sake of love. The days there were like a dream. People only needed to immerse themselves in their ideals without competition, and everything needed would be provided by the government with high quality. Some people wanted to escape from such days, while others wanted to stay.

Julia was back. She was very clear about her inner choices and understood that her mission was not yet complete. Although the places outside of Palm County were full of twists and coldness, as well as many pressures, this was the inevitable path to a fulfilling life. How can one truly appreciate happiness without experiencing hardships? This is what Julia has concluded. Because in the last two months in Palm County, she vaguely felt a bit bored. Those days it seemed more suitable for elderly people who were retired. Their bodies have gradually lost their mobility, no wonder most of the people staying in Palm County were older. But for young people, navigating through the magnificent jungle of life, getting injured, and then healed, is part of a complete life. **We always want to escape from suffering, harm, and the unknown, but we do not realize that these are also part of happiness. Some people only want happiness. But without pain, happiness becomes meaningless. Pain and joy together form a truly happy life.**

向前跑的时候，不要向后看；
向上飞的时候，不要向下瞧。

1. 温柔的母亲

## 1.温柔的母亲

灰黄的天阴冷惨白，预示着一场大雨即将来临，一辆黑色小轿车孤独地行驶在狭窄坑洼的路上。从黄昏时分到夜色降临，车一直在行驶，为了驱散这荒郊野岭的黑暗，司机开启了前照灯。

茱莉亚坐在小轿车后排最中间的位置，眼睛紧盯着车灯前面的路面，空气安静得只听见汽车引擎的声音，身旁是茱莉亚的母亲以及另外一对即将要去巴城参加舞蹈选拔赛的母女。

看着周围匆匆而过的柏树暗影，茱莉亚有种与世隔绝的感觉，仿佛这世界只剩这辆黑色轿车以及车里的五个人了，她看了看周围，母亲和自己一样，盯着前方的路面，司机在认真地开车，每个人都不说话。

一阵莫名的恐惧感袭来，各种关于车祸，被抢劫，被拐卖的不良征兆在脑海里闪现，她又侧着头看了看母亲，母亲只是温和地看着前方，并没有什么情绪写在脸上，茱莉亚用小手握了握母亲温暖的大手，母亲便转过来微笑地看着她，茱莉亚才感到舒心温暖了许多，将头靠在母亲的胸前，摆弄母亲衣物上的小饰品。

"妈，还要多久啊？"茱莉亚看着母亲的眼睛问。

"估计还要 2 个小时。"母亲一如既往温柔地回复着她。

"那今天就不能做作业了，老师留的假期作业。"

"明早早点起来写吧，或者等这次比赛结束回去再写。"

茱莉亚不在说话，忧郁地看着车前方，心里装着来自来自车后方初二年级的作业，以及来自前方即将开始的舞蹈比赛结果的未知，那满腹的担忧让她越发精神，一点困意也没有。

"为什么我总是有写不完的作业？"茱莉亚心里想。

她感受着空气的阴冷和窗外巨大的黑暗，仿佛自己和母亲被世界抛弃了，她想哭，却因为害羞而强行忍住了泪水。


第二天的舞蹈比赛上，茱莉亚穿着粉色的民族服装，耳旁别了一朵大红花，额头上还贴着一个红色的菱形亮片，准备的舞蹈是傣族的孔雀舞。她精湛的舞技赢得了评委的认可，最终拿了一个二等奖。

比赛结束后，茱莉亚和母亲坐在咖啡厅里吃香蕉派，这是她第一次吃香蕉派，奇怪的香味让她有些作呕，因此在香蕉派上咬了一小口，就全部丢给了母亲。可母亲却津津有味吃得很香，茱莉亚突然觉得有些无聊，旋即又想起了还没完成的作业，以及班主任总是严厉的眼神，就更加失去了胃口，她坐在那里，忧郁中带有一丝焦虑地看着周围的人。

"妈，我们什么时候回家？"茱莉亚撅着嘴带着撒娇的语气问母亲。

"买了明天的票。"母亲说，此时香蕉派竟然被母亲全部吃掉了。

"那接下来我们去哪？"茱莉亚继续问。

"去买点东西，这里的柿子饼很有名，我们带回去一些送亲戚。"

茱莉亚不说话，仍然撅着嘴，脸上的青春痘清晰可见，从9岁起，也是她刚开始学舞蹈的那一年，就一直与青春痘形影不离。说是青春痘，实际是由于经常画舞台妆，对化妆品的过敏反应。她本不该在这个粘结频繁地化舞台妆，可无奈为了热爱与艺术，只能牺牲茱莉亚娇嫩的皮肤。因此从9岁开始，她就不知道光滑的皮肤长在自己脸上是什么样子，她讨厌坑坑洼洼的脸，可她更喜欢跳舞，于是茱莉亚很早就体会到：**世间的荣耀只是一场交易，你牺牲了一样，才能获得另一样**。就像她喜欢舞蹈，就要接受练基本功的疼痛、无聊，以及舞台妆对皮肤的伤害。


连续几天的雨夹雪后，窗外出现了阳光，此时正值下午，阳光照在路面的水洼里，房檐的融冰上，街头的积雪处，使得整个街道看起来珊珊可爱。看着这番景象，茱莉亚也突然来了兴致，紧簇的眉头终于有些舒展

　　"妈，那我们走吧，去买特产。"

　　"走吧。"

　　说罢，母亲便买了单，带着茱莉亚出门打车赶往目的地的农贸市场。

## 2.寺庙去哪了？

县城里最近出现了一宗怪事，一些建筑物经常会奇奇怪怪的消失，比如昨天还矗立在马路中间的寺庙，今天再去看，却只剩下了广场，曾经的黄色外墙寺庙似乎从未出现过一般，凭空消失。

这件事不仅惊动了警局，也惊动了市里，市长派人来调查，大批的记者前来采访报导，所有人都在空旷的广场上团团转，没有人知道一幢硕大的建筑去了哪里。

"没给和尚打电话吗？"记者杰恩问街头的大爷。

"嗨，你不知道这寺庙有个规矩，就是拒绝任何电子设备，所以寺里的僧人啊，都没电话，谁也联系不上。"大爷将双手插进袖口里乐呵呵地回答访问的记者。"俺们这个县城吧，压根儿就没什么电话，不发达，但是俺们人民都习惯啦，不影响生活。"

"啊？"记者杰恩的语气有些惊讶："没有通讯设备那多影响生活啊？"

"没啥影响的，小伙儿你不知道，俺们这个县吧，节奏慢，也没啥现代化的设备，但是好就好在在地儿也不大，大家也都不赶时间，平日里的肉蛋粮油，本地都能自产自销了，再加上当地人都没啥大的追求，因此也没觉得生活有什么可值得提高的，更没什么重要到需要加急的事儿。"

记者杰恩的眼里充满难以置信，他将镜头转了一圈，周围也都有楼房和新式建筑，并不荒凉，街面布置甚至颇具艺术美和时尚感，可是大爷的话就像是这里是个不通人烟的山沟，而不是一个现代化的县城。

突然天上一声巨大的轰隆响声，记者杰恩抬头看着天，艳阳高照的天空上只有悠悠的几朵白云，这样的大晴天怎么会有雷声？他仰着头琢磨不出所以然，便去问大爷：

"这样打雷经常出现吗？"

大爷的脸上露出调皮中带有一丝神秘的笑容："不经常出现，今天刚巧被你赶上了。我们当地人的习俗是说有龙王路过，给你捎喜讯来了，所以说啊，今儿个你运气好，说不定一会儿有好事发声。"

正在此时又一声巨大的雷声轰鸣，声音之大记者觉得自己的耳朵都开始嗡嗡作响。正在此时，晴朗的天空果然掠过一道黑影，看来大爷说得没错，天上是有什么物体存在。但不见得是大爷说得龙王，记者杰恩从业多年，虽然也见到一些新奇事件，但是他是个实践主义者,没有亲眼见到的真相,他绝不相信。可是巴城最近发现的离奇事件,使他不得不打破了自己的信条,他开始隐隐觉得这里有些诡异,离奇失踪的寺庙,晴天里的巨大雷声和黑影,以及眼前大爷淡然又诡异的微笑,这一切让他有些脊背发凉,可是又激起了他巨大的探索欲和好奇心。

"如果真有什么神秘力量存在,那么这篇报导必然成为头条。"

想到这里,他突然来了兴趣,打算在小镇长住几天,直到把事件真相挖掘出来为止。

### 3.美丽的小城

茱莉亚又开始不耐烦起来。

此刻她看着在菜场认真挑挑拣拣的母亲，又开始觉得烦闷无聊，14 岁的青春期女孩，对任何事物都带有天然的敌意，无来由的想抵制一切，她拉了拉母亲的衣袖。

"差不多就行了，妈。"

"不要急，你没发现这里的水果蔬菜都很新鲜吗？"

茱莉亚平时只负责吃，哪里有未经加工过的蔬果是否新鲜的概念，她瞟了一眼蔬果摊，发现这上面的果蔬确实色泽鲜艳，个头儿大，紧实饱满仿佛一个个会说话的小胖子。茱莉亚又抬头看了看摊主，发现这些卖家也都是和颜悦色很幸福的样子，他们长得红光满面，完全看不到菜市场果农的辛劳和风尘仆仆在脸上，而是像整天衣食无忧的退休公务员一样神采奕奕。

"你喜欢什么？阿姨可以送给你。"红光满面的菜场阿姨对茱莉亚说。

茱莉亚习惯性地警惕且羞怯地躲到母亲身后，用余光瞟着红光满面的阿姨，茱莉亚是典型的"窝里横"，见到陌生人就变成了"小绵羊"。

"还不说谢谢，你这孩子！"母亲笑盈盈的看着身后的茱莉亚，又转过头来对摊主说："谢谢您了，不用送，我们买一些。"

茱莉亚观察了下周围，好像这个农贸市场并不存在砍价这种事情，每个摊主都很客气友好，来买东西的人也都不占小便宜，双方都尽可能地礼让。

正值下午，外面的太阳躲在巨大的白色云层背后，稀疏地从缝隙露下些许多阳光，房檐上的冰锥溜滴滴答答地向下滴水，菜场里出奇地安静，可以听见水滴敲击水泥路面的声音。茱莉亚看着外面的这一切，她觉得一切似乎都静止了，突然间，一阵温暖美好的感觉袭上心头，她看看可爱又明媚的户外景色，小河里的水哗哩哗啦地流过，街道两旁站立了很多粗壮的树木和姗姗可爱的绿植，她又看看室内，果蔬整齐干净，商贩客气友好。

"这真是个美好的地方啊！"茱莉亚开始感叹起来。

和母亲买完东西去车站的路上，她频频想起刚才在菜场看到的那一幕，觉得自己是不是来到了世外桃源，她和母亲反馈，母亲也说从来没见过这么友好的商贩和新鲜的水果。

出租车司机将两人放在了车站对面，正当母女俩下车，准备进站检票时，却发现来到的地方不是车站，因为她们进了司机指的车站大厅的门，却发现门内空无一人，连检票的机器也没有，什么都没有。

她们从门内退出来，发现写有"巴城火车站"的牌子也不见了。

母女俩觉得难以置信，转过身准备寻找司机，可司机早就开走了，她们又转身看着车站的方向，转过身却发现，刚才还临立的车站，竟然整个消失了。

## 4.巴城中央大街

已经留在巴城一周了，记者杰恩依然毫无头绪，他尝试着从警察这里突破，可是当地警所的警察似乎并不把这件事情放在心上，他们甚至都没有立案，而是将精力放在那些鸡毛蒜皮的小事情上，比如谁家的猫猫走丢了，亦或者谁家的柚子树上的柚子竟然长出了西瓜的皮。

"巴城的超级新闻还真是多啊！"杰恩想："怎么之前从来没发现这么一个神奇的又神秘的地方呢？

这里的女孩很美，是那种自然天然又淡然的美，最可爱的是，她们并不会恃美而骄，对待每个人都客气友好，会用真诚的眼神与你交流，那种清澈的眼神里，你看不到算计和谎言，也看不到忧愁和焦虑，那种美给你一种感觉：就是为自己而美，这令杰恩感到惊讶，并且不是一个女子，他所碰到的每个女子都是这般如

此。可在自己的城市，他从未见过这样的美女，自己城市的女人
的美丽似乎都带着一定的目的性，年轻时她们对男人释放诱惑，
可一旦开始年长成熟，她们的眼神里就多了很多复杂的情绪，露
出野生动物般地冷峻和冷漠。

正在杰恩坐在咖啡馆里沉浸于自己的思考中时，突然被外面
一阵警车的轰鸣声所吸引，他走出咖啡馆望着警车远去的方向，
旋即也启动了自己的小轿车，跟着警车一直来到了一处广场，广
场边缘围了一些人，中间却空无一物，经打听，原来这里曾经是
一个火车站，就在今天下午 3 点 33 分，有人亲眼见到火车站消
失了，报警人是一对母女，此时正在接受警察的安抚和调查。

杰恩走过去看到那对母女，母亲很漂亮，看起来很温柔，从
眼神判断应该是当地的女人，女孩子眼神看起来有些倔强，但是
仍然很清澈，正在他打量这对母女的时候，发现女孩也看向了自
己，杰恩友好地招手跟女孩打招呼，女孩却只是看着他不说话，
仿佛有心事一般。

在安抚过母女俩后，警察将她们安顿在了派出所旁边的一座
旅馆里，但是杰恩有些担心，不知道下一个消失的建筑物会是什
么，似乎整个城市得了一种会失去建筑物的病。已经消失了两处
建筑，这是他有生以来第一次听说，于是他紧随着警察的车，也
来到了母女落脚的旅馆。

杰恩的样子斯斯文文，看起来温和友好，因此女孩母亲很欣
然地答应接受采访。

"小朋友看起来不开心，是不是被吓到了？"杰恩友好地问。

"她老惦记着回家写作业，"母亲轻声细语地回答："这孩子挺上进的，学习成绩也不错。"

"哦，那很好呀，恭喜您有这样的一个好孩子，才艺双全，听说这次还拿了个舞蹈比赛二等奖。"

母亲微笑地低下头看了看女儿，脸上带着笑，眼里带着骄傲的光，

"她还不满意呢，说没拿到第一。"

"已经很好啦，小朋友，"杰恩安慰着女孩说："以后还有很多机会。"

茱莉亚的嘴巴紧闭，眼睛盯着杰恩看了一会儿，突然哇地一声哭了起来，见状两个大人都慌了，母亲赶忙将她揽了过来：

"宝贝，怎么了，是不是被吓到了？"

她用温暖的手轻轻抚着女孩的头。

"妈妈，我们还能回家吗？"女孩的声音啜泣着说。

"很快我们就回家了，你看刚才的警察叔叔和这位大哥哥都是来帮我们的。"

"是的哦，小朋友你不要担心，现在这里休息一晚，明天我们可以去汽车站买张回程的票，坐汽车也一样可以回家的，只是没有火车快。"杰恩说。

听到了两位大人的安慰，女孩开始抽抽噎噎断断续续停止了哭泣。

杰恩觉得心里过意不去，想着女孩这样的状态不适合接受采访，于是早早告辞了母女准备回自己落脚的地方。

正在他起身准备走的时候，再次听到了旅馆外的警车声，旅馆老板和几个面容和睦的人站在门口看着警车的方向。

"怎么了？老板，又发声什么事了。"

老板看着杰恩，不疾不徐地说："听说位于东面的汽车站突然消失了，就连刚进去的乘客也一同不见了。"

杰恩感到巨大的惊讶，他长大了嘴巴，第一次知道惊掉下巴是什么感觉，他回头望着女孩，这次她反倒没哭。"

现在不但这对母女回不去了，自己也回不去了。"杰恩心里想，但此刻更多的，他担心女孩会不会受到更大的惊吓，他看着女孩，她的手紧紧握着母亲的手，好像生怕下一秒母亲也突然消失了。

"你们别担心，我们一定会找到办法送你们回去的。"杰恩说，他虽然说着我们，但是这次他也是一个人来，没有其他同事跟随，他环顾了一下四周，巴城市虽然很好，风景秀美，民风淳朴，可是接连发生的三件怪事也太匪夷所思了，他决定去趟警察局问个究竟。

安抚好母女在这边休息，杰恩便开车前往了警局。

## 5.该去哪里

茱莉亚发现时间好像静止了，原因就是从来到巴城的那天开始，距离她的上个月经期是半个月的时间，而现在已经在这里一个月了，不仅自己没有来月经，母亲也没有。

这一个月她们尝试了各种办法想要离开巴城，无奈巴城只有火车和汽车两种对外的公用交通，于是她们尝试打车，可是司机师傅不跑城外的客单，没有人愿意拉载她们，于是母亲尝试着打电话给家乡的父亲，可是整个县城的电路线都出现了问题，导致对外的电话和对内的通信出不去也进不来。

这可急坏了母女俩，可是好在巴城的政府非常友好，人民也十分亲切，因此在巴城的这一个月，母女俩不仅不需要花钱，还得到了大笔的抚恤金，警察和旅店老板怕母女俩感到烦闷无聊，还经常邀请她们去看各种话剧表演，参加各种当地特色有趣的民俗活动。

正是因为这份友善，逐渐消除了母女俩的恐惧。

到了第二个月的时候，茉莉亚的脸上就时常挂起了孩童该有的纯真笑容，一扫初来时的那种紧张和忧郁，她尽情地享受巴城的生活，与当地的孩子打成一片，没有作业，没有升学压力，也没有各种比赛，她只需要尽情地享受她热爱的事情，无需担心结果。

母亲也尽情享受着当地人直白地赞叹，他们夸母亲美，性格温柔善良，在以前的城市，很少有人如此直接地欣赏母亲，这使得母亲也逐渐爱上了这里，她经常去当地的果园帮果农采摘又大又新鲜的应季当地水果，果农还会付给她一些报酬，有时候是现金，有时候是珠宝首饰，有时候是一些精美的瓷器。

"你们为什么不考虑在这里买栋房子呢？"一位果农大妈对母亲说："这里的房子便宜又宽敞，当地政策十分友好，如果你买了房子，政府还会免费负责装修，用我们最环保的建材和最新款的设计。"

"是挺好的，"母亲说道："可是我们在家乡的城市已经有房子了，我们的房子也很好，孩子的爸爸..."

说到这里，母亲突然停止了。

"孩子的爸爸。"母亲脑海里回忆着家人在一起的温馨时刻，鼻尖感到一阵酸楚。

这两个月的轻松生活，让她一度忘记了远在家乡，还有自己的家人在等待自己回家。

"天呐！"母亲突然开始痛苦起来，双手捂着脸，这是她到了巴城以来第一次哭泣。

一旁的果农大妈连忙上前来安慰：

"不要紧，不要紧，很快就会想到办法回去了，整个政府都在尽最大的努力帮你们。"

"不，不，不。"母亲推开好心上来安慰的大妈："我们，现在，立刻，马上就要走，现在就走！"

说完她站起身，飞快地跑出果园，跑到还在游乐园和一群年轻女孩疯玩的游乐园，拉起女儿的手，就往外走。

"妈，怎么了？怎么这么着急。"

"我们必须得走了，"母亲拉着她的手头也不回地往前走："我们都忘记了最初的目的，在这里耽搁的太久了，你还有作业没写，你忘了吗？"

"可是，妈，我不想再写作业了。"茱莉亚突然挣脱了母亲的手腕，母亲停下来，回头看着女儿。

"妈，我喜欢这里。"茱莉亚脸上洋溢着笑容说，这样孩童般的天真笑容，从她 9 岁开始上小学 3 年级开始，自己就再也没见到过。

"在这里很开心，妈妈。"

母亲看着女儿那一脸的期待，上前抱住女儿，

"可是你不想爸爸了吗？"

"爸爸？"女儿嘴里喃喃了一句，她对这个词感到陌生，自己已经很久没有想到过这个人了，她在母亲的怀抱里安静了好一会儿，抬起头来对母亲说：

"妈，我还是更喜欢这里，我们再呆一段时间吧。"

母亲捋了捋她的头发，点点头，"我们再待一周，你好好的和你的小伙伴们道个别吧。

## 6.时间静止了

杰恩很快就忘记了自己是记者这个身份，因为在这里他找到了自己最热爱的事情，就是陶艺，他整天整天地泡在陶艺馆里，和里面的大师切磋技艺，

很快他就有了自己设计的一套陶艺作品，很快他就成了县城里闻名遐迩的陶艺大师，很快他就开始了自己的第一个陶艺展览，看着络绎不绝的访客，听着连连称赞的鼓励，他的心里升起了一阵荣耀感，他甚至觉得做陶艺是自己来的人世间的使命，只要自己在这里肯付出热情和努力，一定可以做得比大多数人都好。

真不知道自己以前都在干什么，竟然 40 多了，才开始步入陶艺这个行里，想着自己以前的工作，自己以前的工作是什么来着？

一天早上，当他在洗手间面对镜中的自己时，他突然发问，自己以前是干什么的来着？他看着镜中的自己，感到过往的记忆似乎消失了，自己只记得来到这座县城后的自己。

时间好像静止了，杰恩抚摸着自己的鬓角，已经来巴城半年了，这半年来，自己的胡子没有再生长过，自己的脸庞也没有发生任何的变化。他才恍然想起，自己以前好像是个记者来的，是为了调查建筑物消失事件而被派往县城的省级记者。

"啊！"他如梦初醒般大叫了一声。"半年了！"

半年时间竟然就像昨天一样，一晃就过去了。这半年来，消失的车站始终没有出现过，外界也没有人再过来。

他恍然想起，好像还有一对母女来着，和自己同时来到巴城的，不知道她们现在怎么样了。

他开始担心了起来，想起女孩总是忧郁的眼神和那位母亲柔弱的样子。但是旋即他又安下心了，巴城如此温和友善的地方，她们一定是得到了善待。

"应该不用我去操心吧，说不定人家已经回去了。"

想到这里，他又觉得有些不对劲，

"我是不是也该回去了？我以前的生活是什么样子来着？"

种种问题一股脑涌现在杰恩的脑海里，他双手抱着头，觉得大脑发空，他拼命地摇着头，似乎这样就能把消失的信息摇晃出来。

正在此时，天空中传来了一声轰鸣巨响，杰恩赶紧跑到落地窗前，这房子是县城政府奖励他陶艺技术的馈赠，刚接受时，他开心地一夜未合眼。

他向窗外张望，一如既往，晴朗的蓝天，什么也没有。

"难道是我刚刚听错了？"

正在此时，又一声轰鸣巨响，一道黑影从天空飘过。

这场景似曾相识。

杰恩感觉到很难受，未知困惑着他，他跑到门口，换好鞋，推门而出。

## 7.茉莉亚的独白

很小的时候，我喜欢洋娃娃，每次过生日，爸爸就会给我买一个娃娃，很小的时候，是小兔子什么的，大一点了，就是软软的布娃娃，长得很像我，大眼睛大圆脸，再大一点了，爸妈就给我买那种电子会唱歌的洋娃娃，所以我很小的时候就学会了和娃娃讲话，我很孤独，没有兄弟姐妹，她们是我仅有的朋友，因此我特别喜欢她们，帮他们穿衣梳头吃饭，和他们一起入睡。我可以一整天不干别的，专心鼓捣洋娃娃。

后来我好像就有点多动症，我妈就送我去学舞蹈了，那又是另一个世界，最开始我可能就觉得，跳舞可真好看，起始原因是这样的：有一次，我看到一个舞蹈演员，穿着一件红色的舞蹈服装走在校园里，我就被那种美震撼住了，然后我妈就送我去学。

　　真正学习舞蹈后，却发现并不如我所想，学习舞蹈的过程没有那么多的美和浪漫。练基本功很疼，一个动作一个脚步地记忆很慢，不仅动作要到位，还要注意气息和呼吸，这一切和我想象中的完全不同。

　　所以我经常想要放弃，可是母亲不同意，她说做人要有毅力，我那时甚至不懂什么叫做毅力，可是母亲陪我在那里加班练功，我压腿，她看着，我下腰，她吃雪糕，我哭泣，她静静地等待。

　　这种陪伴让我慢慢坚持下来了，直到我获得了县城的一等奖，才发现原来学舞蹈的意义就在于每天一点点的进步，这个过程的艰辛和汗水铸造了最后的荣耀和光芒。从那以后我不再抱怨，每次练功的时候，我都感到一阵平静，压腿微微疼的时候，我都知道一定会涨功，我疼痛，因为我在进步。

　　同样的道理，我后来又喜欢上了很多事物，我爱上了数学，常常考第一，喜欢上了跑步，可以用 5 个小时跑完整场马拉松。这都源自于和母亲共同养成的做事习惯，我从不轻言放弃。

　　并且我懂得了：你在生活中所经历的一些事情，不管是好是坏，它总会翻篇，疼痛，眼泪，荣耀，光芒，都会过去；并且今天别人的苦痛悲欢，明天同样会降临于你。这种感觉让我在波动的人生中保持平静，我觉得没有情绪爱恨情仇的人生，不是完整的人生。

　　我才十几岁，可我却觉得自己懂得了许多的人生道理：人生说到底就是努力地掌控一种随波逐流，一边逐流一边掌控，好的舵手，不会一意孤行，也不会完全听任风浪。

## 7.茉莉亚的独白

　　自我意志与自然意志是相互交织的好友，相互牵制，相互和谐。

　　　　　　　　　　　　-----茉莉亚，记于来到巴城的 6 个月后。

## 8.巴城堡垒

风渐起，乌云越聚越多，天色也越来越暗。

杰恩走在路上，感觉周围的行人越来越少，自己似乎迷路了。尽管这半年来在，他将巴城基本上所有的地方都逛遍了，可眼前的地方他却从未来过。周围的建筑物全部都很有设计感，虽然灰土土的，但是充满力量感。

此番景象令他感到好奇，继续往前走，天空突然出现了几只鸟，又黑又大，还时不时地发出凄厉的惨叫。

应该是乌鸦，杰恩心里想。

头顶上的乌云越聚越多，风也越来越大，他顶着风继续往前走，突然间，眼前出现了一道悬崖，整个地面放佛被齐平地切了一刀，他的心瞬间被提到嗓子眼儿，双腿发麻，看着一脚就会跌下去的空地，站在悬崖边上竟然可以俯瞰整个县城。还好悬崖也不算太高，向下望去，街道房屋排布像梯田一样一阶一层地排列开去，显得温馨美好。

杰恩退后几步，环顾四周，黑压压的天显得触手可及，凄厉惨叫的黑色大鸟们盘旋在乌云之下，越聚越多，崖上崖下，所有的道路都七扭八歪，莫名地，一股悲壮感涌上心头，他也不知道自己怎么会突然产生这样的情感。

自己应该是来到了一座山顶上，且周围还有三三两两的房屋，以及一幢巨大的纪念碑似的建筑。

杰恩逐渐走近纪念碑似的建筑，发现竟然是一个塔型的堡垒，杰恩环绕堡垒走了一圈，赫然发现一个隐藏的地下通道，他向下看去，里面黑黢黢的，彷佛能够吞噬一切，他感到脊背发麻，可是强烈的好奇心还是驱使着他向黑色的地下通道走去。

他从口袋里掏出手机，将手电筒的光亮调至最大，一路沿着地下通道右面的墙壁走了进去。

里面很黑，有点阴冷，但是没有尘土和腐朽的味道，这应该不是一个没人来的地方。他继续往前走，视野逐渐开阔，也依稀地看到了一些花瓶，桌椅之类的器物。

"应该是有人经常来这里打扫的。"杰恩这样想。

前方依然有路，杰恩继续走，随着周围出现的陶瓷字画等器具物件越来越多，他发现前方有一个小广场一样的圆形空地，地面上呈八卦阵一样排开地印有规律排布的符号和文字，看起来像中文，但又有点像甲骨文。

G 点开手机上的翻译软件，将墙壁上的文字照片输入引擎搜索，原来是巴文，一种古老的文字语言，杰恩又将墙壁上的一片文字放入搜索引擎中去翻译，竟然是一首诗：

*人应该做艺术品而不是艺术家。*

*雕琢自己，而不是燃烧自己；*

*滋养自己，而不是压榨自己；*

*宽恕自己，就是放过别人；*

*接纳自己，就会包容世界；*

*心灵和身体都需要锻炼，通过阅读和运动；*

他又将墙壁上其他的几片文字也输入搜索引擎去翻译：

*想赢就要不怕输，想要勇敢就要学会正视懦弱；*

*学会忽视结果，重视过程；*

*学会取舍，在乎主要的，忽略次要的；*

*我写文字希望500年后的我能找到我自己，能看到一个女人在500年前的灵魂香气，有许许多多的我可以沿着优质文学哲学的足迹去找到自己，这是身为一个思想传播者的使命。*

*————女王塞亚琳*

"女王塞亚琳是谁？"杰恩看着最后的落款心中发出了疑问："这是一些做事做人的道理，很有力量感，但不知道是谁留下来的。"

杰恩回过身低下头，看着距自己脚尖不到 1 米的八卦圆圈最外围的边缘，停止了前进。

"要不要踏入这个圆形的八卦阵？"他纠结在原地。

突然，他感到一阵窒息，好像周围的空气不再流通了，紧接着，是一阵眩晕，整个世界天旋地转，他摇摇晃晃，手机意外掉到了地上，照到棚顶，竟然是一副巨大的画，正在惊讶之际，突然眼前一黑，整个人晕了过去。

## 9.众人受益的婚礼

塞亚琳的未婚夫是她父亲战友的儿子，父母对这个准女婿很满意，自己对他也不算讨厌。他长得很胖，鼻下留有小胡子，但面目和善，待人友好，并且在巴国位高权重，家世显赫。

"多少女孩做梦都想挤进去的家族，你可要珍惜。"塞亚琳的哥哥这样对她说。

塞亚琳有一个哥哥，还有一个弟弟，他们对她都很好，从小到大，家里最好的教育资源，最多的成长关注，最多的宠爱都给了塞亚琳这个女孩子。

因此塞亚琳的婚礼，成了巴国最大的喜事，结婚那天，所有的人夹道庆祝，所有的县城明星权贵都到了婚礼现场，所有百姓都赞美与祝福这桩堪称完美结合的婚姻。

见到自己的父母兄弟，自己国家的人民都高兴，说不出由来地，塞亚琳也很开心。

婚后的日子没有什么大的波澜，自从嫁给了现在的丈夫之后，自己家族生意的规模逐渐扩大，哥哥掌管了主要的公司，弟弟在塞亚琳丈夫的资源对接下调配到了中央发展，而塞亚琳的父母也换了更大的房子，每一个人的生活似乎都得到了大幅度的改善和提升。

只是塞亚琳自己经常觉得很枉然，她对自己的丈夫说不上是爱，但也说不出是什么别的感情。有时候她也好奇，爱情是什么？自己似乎从未经历过这一切，就被安排上了一条"最好的道路"，自己结婚后，以前的同学朋友，都来恭喜自己，说自己越来越美了，甚至比以前更年轻。

是的，自己现在不但比以前年轻，还比以前更加富有，由于自己的婚姻，现在父亲在县城的身份相当于县长。

这是一段所有人都受益的婚姻。

夜深人静的时候，塞亚琳经常彻夜不眠，所有人，真的是所有人吗？

在思考了无数个夜晚之后，她提出了疑问：自己，真的是那个受益人吗？

夜深人静的时候，她看着身边熟睡的丈夫，觉得丈夫就像一头猪，简单热情，吃得很多，想得很少。

自己是怎样爱上他的？

等等，自己真的爱过他吗？

爱是什么？

爱情又是什么？

她看着酣睡的丈夫，这个简单的男人，大概永远不会有这样的问题。

可是自己就这样每天面对这样的人啊！

她转过身去，不想看见那只猪的脸，一滴眼泪顺着塞亚琳的眼角流到了枕头上。

"自己怎么会爱这样的人呢？根本就不爱呀！"

找到了答案，她泪流满面，这桩所有人都受益的婚姻，牺牲的只有自己。

"虽然自己集万千宠爱，可自己就是个没有自我意志的宠物，是精致的波斯猫，精美的花瓶，皇冠上最闪耀的宝石，永远乘借外界的庇护和光芒。"

她越哭越凶，枕头逐渐被晕湿了一大片，灵魂一旦觉醒，便再难以安定。

于是在第二天早晨，她逃离了巴国，只留下了一张自己要去寻找自由和真爱的纸条。

塞亚琳的家人急坏了，尤其是母亲，女儿从小到大从来都很听话，突然间的离家出走让母亲一病不起。

正在此时，战争爆发了，塞亚琳的哥哥、弟弟、丈夫还有父亲，作为巴国的核心人物，全部被卷入了战争。

战争极其激烈和残酷，对方的军力火力是巴城的几十倍，很快这里便尸横遍野，残暴的敌军不仅袭击了热爱和平的巴城，甚

至不放过普通百姓，在占领了巴国三个月后，对军对此地进行了
屠城。

　　他们将巴国人的尸骨堆积在一座堡垒上，可是尸体越来越臭，
发出来的腐臭味引来了周围大批成群的乌鸦和秃鹫，于是敌军放
了几把火，烧了三天三夜，将所有巴国的尸体全部烧光，焚烧的
过程中，火光噼里啪啦地发出凄厉的叫喊，像成千上万巴国的人
民的嘶喊和挣扎。

## 10.何时回家?

茱莉亚在巴城的半年觉得很开心,在这里没有课业压力和同学们间略为复杂的人际相处,她感受到前所未有的自由,只是这半年来,自己的身体一直没有生长,也没有发育,这急坏了她的母亲。

母亲一直想要带自己回家,可是在茱莉亚一味的坚持下,还是拖延到了半年。过去这半年,茱莉亚感到的不仅仅是身体上的自由:她可以随意的跳舞,去山野间像个疯丫头一样肆意奔跑,以及不受拘束地和县里的任何一个人聊天攀谈任何内容。

她还享受着精神上的绝对自由,这里的每一个人都鼓励支持她做任何事,这让她觉得自己就是高高在上的小公主。虽然以前她在家里就是个小公主,爸爸妈妈爷爷奶奶外公外婆都把她捧在手心儿里,他们应允自己的各种无理取闹,可是爷爷奶奶外公外婆都离世很早，他们离世后，父母整天忙于生意，就很少像小时候那样陪伴自己了。

可是在巴城，有更多人爱自己，包容自己，她觉得好像小时候那样，充满爱意的，被关注的日子又回来了。所以茱莉亚舍不得离开，甚至想将自己的爸爸也接过来。

"起床了吗，我的小猪？"随着一阵敲门声，和妈妈温柔的轻唤，母亲走进了茱莉亚的卧室。

茱莉亚裹着被子勉强支撑着坐立在床上，睡眼惺忪地看着母亲对自己说：

"快点去洗漱，今天我们要回家！"

"妈妈，真的吗？"

"什么真的吗？"

"你说过接爸爸过来，见到爸爸我们就回来。"

"真的，真的，你快去洗脸刷牙。"

听罢这句话，茱莉亚才从床上跳下来。

今天的天气不是很好，巴城少见的乌云密布，看起来要下雨的样子，茱莉亚和母亲走在路上，并没有带很多东西，她观察着母亲的脸，母亲双唇紧闭，认真地往前走去，看来这次母亲是下定决心要带茱莉亚离开巴城，但不知母亲想到了什么样的离开方式没有。

这半年里，母亲尝试用各种各样的方法离开。

火车站消失了，他们就去汽车站，汽车站不见了，他们就尝试坐出租车，可是没有一个出租车司机愿意载她们离开，他们都只接巴城内部跑车的生意。虽然这段日子茱莉亚感到很快乐，可是母亲却很绝望，母亲觉得巴城好虽好，（没错这里思想自由，阳光明媚且物质丰盛）可毕竟不是自己的家乡，母亲还惦记着茱莉亚的父亲和其他亲人，尽管自己的家乡并不完美（民风彪悍且野蛮），可那毕竟是自己的家乡啊！

这半年来母亲一直尝试着和外界联系，可是这里似乎和外界断了往来，再也没看到有巴城外的人进来，就在母亲感到没路了，绝望之际，突然想到了共同来巴城的杰恩。这半年来，不知道记者杰恩怎么样了，于是在电话簿上找到了杰恩，几人约好今天在巴城最西边的喷泉广场见面。

此时母亲已经带着女儿到了喷泉广场，可是却不见往日的喷泉，取而代之的是一座堡垒，堡垒上方黑压压地盘旋着数十只乌鸦，这场景令母亲和茱莉亚都感到脊背发凉。

"妈妈，我们回去吧，我害怕。"茱莉亚哆嗦着拉着母亲的手。

"别怕，妈在呢！"

母亲牵着茱莉亚的手，曾几何时母亲也是见到什么都怕的小女孩，可是自从女儿的出生，自从母亲的母亲的离世，她自己就成为了可以承担一切的"母亲"，在任何时候，尤其是儿女面前，'母亲'都不能害怕。

母亲拉着女儿的手，绕着堡垒走了一圈，才发现一个通往地下的洞，她想着要不要下去探个究竟，或许离开巴城的玄机就在这个通道里。

就在母亲犹豫之际，茱莉亚已经先行向地下通道走了过去。

"茱莉亚，你回来！"母亲惊恐地喊道。

女儿回过头，看着妈母亲说："妈妈，我知道你在想什么，我们下去看看吧，这次我们一定要回家。"

母亲看了看女儿，发现女儿稚嫩的小脸上开始有成熟懂事的神态，这更加坚定了母亲要回去的想法，她要让女儿过正常人的人生，哪怕充满风雨，可是那是一个女孩成长的必经之路。并且外面的世界不管有多少艰险，自己都会陪女儿度过，但是女儿不能够停留在这里停止了生长。

想到这里母亲的眼眶湿润了，她走到茱莉亚前面将女儿拉往身后，

"跟在妈妈身后。"

## 11.二次屠城

十年后，塞亚琳已经成为了东方某个中型国家的女王，她不仅有了自己的军队，还有了新的丈夫和自己的孩子。

当拥有了这一切的塞亚琳返回巴国，发现昔日的建筑物，家人和人民都不见了，并且巴国也改名了赛亚国。并且从当地百姓那里得知，巴国在 10 年前自己的离家出走之后，就被屠城的消息后，她悲愤地口吐鲜血，为曾经任性的自己感到自责，为不能够对曾经的家人尽到职责感到懊悔，更为敌人的残暴感到怒火中烧。

于是塞亚琳召集了自己在中型小国所建立的军队，攻打赛亚国。

女王塞亚琳的军队骁勇善战，全部都是孔武有力，智勇双全的年轻人，因此很快便俘获了塞亚国的国王和军队。

同样的手段，女王塞亚琳也对塞亚过进行了屠城，赛亚国的人有的被活埋在城堡之下，有的被焚烧在城堡之中。

二次屠城之后这，女王塞亚琳找回自己曾经居住的房子，以及焚烧尸体的堡垒。她将堡垒重新修建，并在堡垒上刻上了所有曾经巴国人民的名字。

堡垒修建好后，一切就像从未发生过一样，可是在堡垒上方，人们总能看到成群结队的乌鸦在盘旋，似乎在寻找期待着什么。

随着女王在中型国家的政治地位逐渐提高，塞亚琳最终统治了中型国家，并将巴国指定为中型国家附属国，改名巴城。由于对家乡和逝去亲人的深切怀念，她赋予了巴城独立的经济和政治政策，将中型国家最好的资源导入巴城，并且在巴城制定了最好的政府福利，只有在中型国家最优秀，最有道德和才华的人才，才能够拥有巴城居民身份。

此时，杰恩突然睁开了双眼，他看着周围，梦里屠城的情节吓得他一身冷汗，他看了看周围，散发着腐朽的味道，没错，是腐朽的味道，难道这就是当初被屠城焚尸的堡垒，而刚才的梦，就是巴城的发展历史？而自己进来堡垒时看到的纪念碑上的文字，就是成千上万巴城，哦不，巴国人民的姓名。

冰冷的风咆哮在堡垒之外，仿佛充满怨恨的呐喊，要将整个世界撕成碎片。此情此景，杰恩的内心受到了极大的触动，回忆起梦中屠城百姓脸上狰狞痛苦的表情,杰恩感到心脏剧烈的疼痛,他捂住心脏的位置,开始哭泣。

突然,他感受到眼前一阵光亮,抬头一看,发现眼前站着一个身着白衣的女人;定睛细看,觉得如此熟悉;杰恩又仔细瞧了瞧,觉得好像在哪里见过眼前的女子,恍然间想起,这不就是刚刚在梦里的女王塞亚琳。

正是梦中的女王塞亚琳!

他感到惊讶不已,一时间分不清自己现在是梦是醒。

此刻,眼前的白衣女人正在朝他微笑。

## 12.母亲的独白

逐渐步入中年，我发现身边的很多女人，是很厉害的。她们不差钱，能力强，人也美，生几个孩子都行，大抵人到了中年老年，不出意外都会这样吧，拥有一堆孩子，和一个只剩亲情的老公，再或者，老公中途毁约，只剩孩子或者失去孩子。

可在我的概念里，没有爱情和温暖理解彼此的另一半，要那么多钱有什么用？一个女人，有一个小孩，一个人带，不是也很无聊么？人活着不就是感知感恩于各种关系，并在这些关系里纠织。

我看那些修行的，学佛的，跟我讲怎么怎么好，超脱自在的，可我想我来到人世间之前，应该早就知道世间不好，生命总是痛，所以才选择纷纷扰扰的红尘。**只有欢乐的人生，该多么轻，就像灵魂不曾依附于肉身，意识流一样存在于大气之中。**

似乎人生怎么选择都是有代价，大家都痛，谁也别嘲笑谁。

因此女儿就像我的第二次生命，我爱她胜于我自己，她是我的作品，是我布满痛苦和无聊的人生中的光亮出口。

回忆过往，我的人生有高光有低谷，而此时我已不再像年轻时候那样，会为了许多事情大动情感。

我曾对自己说：假如有一天知道自己要赢，我就坚定地去走，不悲伤不心急；假如有一天我知道要输，我还是坚定地去走，因为结果已成定数。

以前我总是想赢，碰到比赛就血液沸腾，可是现在这种感觉淡去了许多。我经历过，更加懂得社会上每一个看起来好的坏的人，都不容易，都有自己的逻辑体系，无论他在别人眼里多么坏，在他自己那里都是正确的。与其批判，我更想接纳人性。

夏天的蝉，总是叫得人耳鸣，它们隐藏在不知道哪里，热浪一来，疯狂咆哮，对于蝉来说，鸣叫一个夏天，死去，全部的蝉生意义结束了。像极了人生的缩影，在最热烈的人生年华，叫嚷着，消耗着，随着秋风渐起声音愈低，生命油尽灯枯。

生命是场体验，别人羡慕的，未必适合我，别人厌弃的，未必让我觉得难过。人可怜的向上帝祈求一点意义和存在感，可这些最后都像土耳其的地毯一样被卷走，更有可能，被践踏。因此道德经说：水善利万物而不争，处众人所恶，故几于道。

我的女儿，她总是和3这个数字有不不解之缘，她出生于1992年3月3日晚上六点十分，做事情喜欢保持在3、6、9这样的单数。她对轨迹尤其敏感，不小心向左转了个圈，一定要向右再转回来。没事就在本本上画轨迹图，说要给我算命，每到这时我都哭笑不得。

她很是聪明，听过的东西几乎从来不会忘，很擅长记忆情节类的东西。我觉得她的这些特质第一适合炒股：做图+编故事；第二适合写作。因此我很重视对她的教育，也很重视对她的特长培养。

女儿很贴心，她也很爱我，但是她大多数时候都任性且有主见，谁也制服不了她，她总爱和爸爸辩论，小嘴巴很会说。

我很珍惜和女儿在一起的每一刻，眼神总是离不开她。有的时候我也会伤感，我的宝贝，将来要嫁给什么样的人。以前我总期待她要嫁给真正的爱情，嫁给她最爱的人啊，嫁给第一眼很完美先生，我现在仍然这样期待。

因为我知道，相比于被爱，爱人其实更幸福，我希望我的女儿，有源源不断自己制造幸福，创造爱的能力，我希望她是太阳，是恒星，自己发光发热，而不是乘借别人的光芒。

我的宝贝，这漫长的人生，妈妈不能陪你一辈子，一个好的人生伴侣是很重要的，愿你将来有温馨和谐的家庭，不要为了任何一项单一的事物而贡献一生，而是完完整整的做个平凡人，平稳安心的度一生，努力地尽到义务，体验生命，如果有幸，站得更高些，也不错。

总之，女儿，我希望你是独立完整又强大的个体，而我们，爱你的人，会永远围绕着你，护你前行，欣赏你的光芒。

--------母亲

## 13.齐聚一堂

刚才的梦到底是怎么回事？盛大的婚礼，战争，屠城，堡垒，这些都是真的吗？杰恩感到大脑一阵混乱，刚想开口问，就见眼前白衣女子开口说话了：

"没错，你梦境里的一切都是真实发生过的。"

杰恩惊得一身激灵，打了个哆嗦，用难以置信的眼神看着白衣女子问：

"你就是那个塞亚琳？那个离家出走后回来屠城的女王塞亚琳？"

"对，我就是她，"塞亚琳回答到，一抹神秘的笑容挂上了嘴角：

"只不过这一切都发生在 999 年前。"

杰恩咽了下口水，巨大的震惊使他讲不出话来。

"你现在脑子里一定充满了疑问，为什么一千年了我仍然在这里，刚刚的梦境有几分是真的，消失在巴城的建筑物到底是怎么回事。"

虽然自己只字未讲，但塞亚琳好像有看透人灵魂的能力，杰恩努力的掐了掐自己的大腿内部，真实的疼痛感让他知道自己眼前的这一切并不是假的，他连忙起身，朝着白衣女子拜了拜。

"那么您一定是巴城的祖先，就是人们口中经常提到的女王塞亚琳，就是您缔造了整个城市。"

塞亚琳看着俯首叩拜的杰恩，嘴角挂起了满意的笑容：

"是的，我就是建立了整个县城的，人民口中的女王塞亚琳。只是很久很久以前，这里还没什么人，这个县城位于过境边界，曾几何时是一个独立的小国，我的父亲和丈夫，是近乎国王一般的存在，后来这里发生的一切，就如你梦境中那样。"

"可是您为什么要逃离巴城，不，是巴国，逃离后来为什么又回来？"

塞亚琳看着杰恩笑了笑，似乎早就料到他会问这个问题，

"这是一个困扰了千年的问题，每一个来到这里的新人都会问的问题。"

"每一个？"

"是的，其实巴城的大部分人，甚至说绝大部分人都是外来人口，曾经组建新家园的那一批人都是我的部下，他们现在早就离世了，如果单凭那几个人的后代，巴城早就消失了。"

"都像我一样的外来人口吗？"

"我先来回答你的第一个问题，你不要着急，我们一个一个问题来，我都会回答你的，请你不要趴在地上了，坐到这边的桌子旁，我们一会儿还有新的客人。"

"新的客人？"

正在此时，耳旁传来了一阵刺耳的尖叫，杰恩转头一看，是半年前的小女孩，茉莉亚看着眼前通体发光的白衣女子，发出了恐怖的尖叫，旁边是她的母亲，看来他们也梦到了杰恩刚进入地下堡垒前所梦见的一切。

"你，你是那个女王塞亚琳？"女孩惊恐着发问，紧接着看向杰恩说道："你是今天要带我们离开的叔叔？"

## 14.女王的发言

"很多人都曾经问我，为什么如此好的日子，如此好的家人，我还总是不知足，我逃离了巴国是不是因为早早地预知了这里即将发生的一切？而我的回答是'不是'。我并不知道这里即将要发生的一切，而我离开巴国，离开我所深爱的家人，只是因为，我从来没有体验过，强烈和深刻的爱是一种什么感觉。我不是说别人对我，而是我对别人。我不是单指对人类，就算是对某样事物，都某种爱好，我也没有体验过，什么叫做热爱。

在离开巴国之前，我拥有近乎完美的人生，我的父亲视我为掌上明珠，我的哥哥弟弟舍命守护着我，母亲是我最贴心的姐妹，丈夫对我忠诚且疼爱有加，世界上最珍奇的宝物，最完美的情谊，最忠诚的守候，最温柔的呵护，我统统都有，我就像爱和荣耀的承载者，即便你翻看历史书籍，也鲜有拥有这一切的公主。"

讲到这里，塞亚琳停顿了下，对面桌前坐着的三人已经听得如痴如醉。

"说来好笑，我逃离，是因为我不曾体会痛苦。许多人觉得这不可思议，怎么会有人去主动寻求痛苦？可有一种你们无法体会的的痛苦，叫做没有痛苦，**因为没有痛苦，就没有欢乐，没有强烈的痛苦，就无法产生坚定的幸福。**我想我的父母兄弟和丈夫，他们都有这样的体验，为了守护我，他们饱经风霜，尝遍苦难，他们是幸福的，而我却永远只得承受这沉甸甸的'爱'的给予。这让我无法感知爱，不再了解爱，甚至我开始憎恨讨厌我的丈夫，觉得嫁个他是一切错误的开始。"

塞亚琳看着母亲，母亲抿了抿嘴角，想到自己在来到巴城之前，也是有着同样的体会，她是和丈夫（也就是茱莉亚的父亲）大吵了一架后，才带着茱莉亚来到巴城参加比赛的。

塞亚琳继续说道：

"于是我逃离了丈夫，来到了中型国家的首都。在那里，没人知我我是公主还是女皇，他们像普通人一样对待我，我在那里接受教育，在那里参加工作，又在那里组建自己的团队，逐渐地我在中型城市越来越有声望，并且靠自己的能力赚取了大量的财富，我觉得这一切的获得是那样幸福，他们靠我自己，而不是我的父母兄弟和丈夫。

就在我荣归故里，期待和家人一同分享这些是时刻，发现故乡的一切早已不见了，野蛮的塞亚人屠杀了我所有百姓，包括我的父母兄弟。愤怒激发了我的仇恨，于是我像男人那样，亲自当首领，指挥军队，打败了塞亚人，用相同的方式屠杀了他们所有的人民，就在这里，就在你们所在的这座堡垒里，大火一次一次，烧了我的子民，和他们的全部人民。"

听到这里，桌边坐着的三位现代人面面相觑，面前的白衣女子不仅是温柔宽厚的巴城女神，更是快意恩仇的塞亚琳女皇，可以温柔似水，可以坚忍果决，更可以驰骋疆场，对敌人痛下杀手。

一阵庄严敬意肃然在整个堡垒内部升腾了起来。

"战争之后，我重新建立了巴城，带着我从中型国家征服的团队和军队，让巴城附属于中型国家，让我曾经的国家做个安居乐业的地方小县，并且将中型国家最好的资源和政策导入巴城，单独起草了一份治国方案。"

## 15.女王箴言二十一条

1.哪里有灵魂，哪里就有光明。

2.人生是一场游戏，只有先顺应规则，才有机会凸显自己。

3.行动和过程就是报应本身，也是回报本身。

4.改变应该是基于骨子里的羞耻感，而不是谁的道德绑架。

5.人都会变老，强者要懂得给弱者空间。

6.不能用理性去对抗感性。

7.心里有爱，就会对一切宽容。

8.没有一个人可以占尽上帝的光辉，人们应该相互尊重。

9.站在泡沫上的希望没价值。

10.阳光就算不照在你这里，也会照在别人那里，不如主动去追寻阳光。

11.自己长得丑，就要把镜子打碎吗？

12. 人生没有了喜欢的事物，除了炫耀就是炫耀。

13. 群众的眼光是瞎子。

14. 心应当有根，这样漫漫人生路便不会随波逐流；心应当有脚，这样众多大路中才能选择出自己的路。

15. 不要陪死去的人一起死，要陪活着的人好好活。

16. 有能力改变命运后就要自己发光。

17. 像爱你的人爱你那样爱自己。

18. 物不为我所有，物为我所用。

19. 当你全部放下外界，才能全部遵从自我。

20. 大部分女人想结婚，生孩子，不是她骨子里就想要的，而是世俗的任务和基于爱的责任感裹挟。

21. 幸福是快乐和痛苦的结合体，有些人将幸福单纯地解释成快乐，是片面的，因为存在快乐就一定存在痛苦，就像黑夜和白天：如果没有黑夜，就不存在白天了。幸福的程度取决于支配快乐和痛苦的能力，因为快乐和痛苦都是人生所无法避免的，因此能够控制自己的快乐和痛苦显得尤为重要。

## 16.赛亚琳的马

我来到中型国家的那一年，刚好 23 岁，同年我开始寻找工作，很顺利地，我进入了一家马场负责财务工作，老板见我聪明好学，很快便将他所有的马场财务都交由我来打理，不到一年时间我便掌握了马场的经营之道。

24 岁那一年我便同几位同僚出来创业，经营起了自己的小马场。

25 岁，马场经营的还不错，我有了小金库，于是又去了两个大型国家考察学习。

27 岁我将马场规模扩大，并在大型国家设立了分公司。

28 岁，我将马场的产业链扩充至金融，提供马匹租赁，因此开始了和军队合伙做生意，也在此时认识了我的第二任老公。

29 岁，由于战争，我的马匹大量的被军队所需要，我在军队的声誉逐渐显赫。

30 岁，我近乎拥有了自己军队，与马相关的业务，都需要来找我。

31 岁，我将马匹事业扩展至科技，提供更先进精良的坐骑出行工具。

32 岁，许多活不下去的小马场甚至是小型国家臣服于我，希望我收购并接济他们。

33 岁，中型国家授予我最高荣耀，我拥有相应的军队权力和财政大权。

34 岁，我带着这一切荣归故里，却发现，我曾经圈养的精良马匹，亲自踏碎了我的家乡。

后面的一切如你们所梦见。

中型国家的三大产业链：马匹，金融，科技；在此之外，文艺链条发达。而我在经商的这 10 年，恰恰好的布局了这些产业核心命脉。

"那么消失的车站是怎么回事？这里的通信设施是怎么回事？还有你们的人民，虽然很好，但看起来和外界人民格格不入。"杰恩发问到。

"车站没有消失，是它本来就不曾存在。"塞亚琳脸上挂起了一抹神秘的笑容："能来到这里的人，都是我们通过大数据精挑细选的人。"

塞亚琳一挥手，只见身后的幕布落下，透明的玻璃罩后面是成百上千个带着蓝牙耳机在操弄电脑的 IT 人士。

"巴城的 IT 技术无人能及，但是我们不想因为通讯的发展而影响了人民的生活质量，因此外部保持着最原始的生活模式，我们的蔬果是全世界虽新鲜的，我们的水是全世界最清甜的，我们的人民，你们在赛亚县所看到的每个人，个个身怀绝技，且深藏不露。"

看着埋头工作的几百号 IT 科技人员，以及大屏幕上的数据，三人瞠目结舌。

"那为什么会选上我们来巴城呢？我们并没有身怀什么绝技，只是普通百姓罢了，现在我们只想回去。我们还有自己的生活，不想终身被困在这样一个巴掌大的小城。"年轻的母亲说到这里，留下了眼泪。"每个人都有选择自己生活的权利，待在这里不是我们想要的！"

朱莉亚看见哭泣的母亲，赶忙上前安慰。

"是啊，为什么选择我们呢？"杰恩也问到："那么多人怎么就选中了我们？"

## 17.强悍的生命力

女王塞亚琳转身走到玻璃门旁边，按下了一个按钮，巨大的玻璃幕瞬间变成了墙壁，刚才忙碌的工作人员消失在眼前，她又按下了门旁边的另一个按钮，只见墙壁变成了中央火车站的样子。

车站上上下下人来人往，很热闹的样子。

"每一个新来到赛亚市的人，都会经历你们所经历的一切；每一个公民也都有选择离开，或是回来的权利，这是这座县城守护者们赋予你们的自由。"

"太好了！那我们什么时候可以离开？"母亲问。

"随时，我今天就送你们离开，只是离开这里后，关于这里的一切，都将消除在你们的脑海里，你们将忘记这里的一切，彻底回到原来的生活。"

听到这些，茱莉亚有些犹豫，母亲也有些动容。

"可是为什么会选择我们呢？"杰恩问："我的意思是你们的数据库里这么多人，为什么偏偏选择了我们当公民标本。"

"其实我不是塞亚琳，只是她的继承人。"白衣女子说："但是你们可以叫我塞亚琳，因为她的每一任继承人都叫塞亚琳，我是从众多克隆体中被筛选出来最适合当继承人的个体。之所以选择你们，是因为你们极其的纯粹，善良，充满爱且才华横溢。在我们的大数据库中，网罗着所有人的信息和经历，对他们的性格以及基因的分析指数，使得我们筛选出了你们。"

坐着桌旁的三个人不淡定了，一种被监控的恐惧使得他们毛骨悚然，杰恩刚想开口说什么，却被塞亚琳抢先说道：

"你一定觉得，如此大规模的数据，我们如何做到？此番的操控是否合乎情理？我们是否侵犯了你们的人身权利？"

塞亚琳的目光扫过在座的每一个人，先是到母亲身上，

"你长久以来想要逃离婚姻，可是因为孩子和父母而无法离开丈夫，你爱着丈夫，甚至和他的性格并不适合做夫妻，你仍然尽心尽力服侍他，现在我们给了你一次重新选择的机会。"

她的目光又停留在了茱莉亚身上，

"你讨厌无休止的作业和功课，喜欢跳舞，我们之所以给你二等奖，是因为中国的易经八卦里的一卦：亢龙有悔。物极必反，怕你骄傲，怕你承担不住冠军荣耀所带来的反噬，希望你永远向上且自律。"

塞亚琳的目光最终落在杰恩的身上，说道：

"你在这里不是实现了你想要的一切，你的理想，你想要的轻松生活？"

三个人面面相觑，一时间不知道说什么好。

塞亚琳继续说道："现在我给你们一次重新选择的机会，你们当然可以回去，但你们要想好：你所想要的是对现实的妥协？是基于寻求安稳的懦弱？还是真正对于你和后代未来的思考？**你当然可以选择回去，你也可以选择回来，你甚至可以选择这世界任何一个地方，只是不要被恐惧阻碍了脚步，被亲人限制了发展，被传统固封了疆界，被权威左右了思想。**"

这一番言论深深触动了在座几个人的心弦，三个人面面相觑望着彼此。

"你们现在就可以作出选择，选择留下的，你可以在这里拥有公民身份，可以拥有你想要的人生；选择离开的，我们的鹏鸟会送你们回家，你仍然会拥有你想要的人生。

## 18.回归

塞亚琳的脸上带着微笑说道，她的目光扫过茱莉亚，扫过母亲，停留在了杰恩的身上。

"我，我选择留下来，"杰恩说道："巴城就像一个美好的世外桃源，我从小就在课本上学到过有乌托邦的桃源生活，没想到有生之年真的来到了这样的地方，我想这样的生活是千千万万个人的梦，所以我想继续下去，留在这里，成为这里的一份子，为女王你效力。"

塞亚琳面带微笑点了点头，又将目光转移到了母亲的身上，母亲看了看女王塞亚琳，又看了看女儿，她来到女儿面前，半蹲在她身前，轻柔地问女儿：

"宝贝，妈妈问你，你喜欢跳舞吗？"

女儿的眼睛看着妈妈不说话。

"妈妈的意思是，你跳舞开心吗？"

"也不是一直都开心，但是大部分时候开心。"

"那你愿意一直选择这条路吗？一直为了你热爱的事情去奋斗努力？"

女儿思考着，不知该作何回答，她知道妈妈是想回家的。

"你不要考虑妈妈，"妈妈似乎看出了她的心思："妈妈百分百尊重你的选择，从小到大，只要你喜欢的，妈妈都全力支持，妈会把能找到的最好资源给你铺路，妈妈还会陪着你。"

看着妈妈，茱莉亚回想着自己懂事以来的经历，她想到自己先天柔韧性差，腰硬的像钢板，别的小朋友已经可以横叉竖叉了，她的前腿后腿才刚刚能搭在把杆上90度。别的小朋友已经能走前桥后桥了，她才勉强能下个腰。舞蹈这条路并不适合她。

茱莉亚又想到在自己的家乡，自己的数学总是满分，自己写的作文总是被老师当成范文来读，大家都叫自己才女，她想起在小学中学的荣耀，想起怎么也攻克不下的舞蹈，也许就是一种不服输，让她在舞蹈上大下功夫，也许就是因为舞蹈比赛可以让她看到不同的世界，从小镇到省会，再到京都，她才喜欢舞蹈，说到底她爱的还是荣誉感和五彩斑斓的世界，想到这里，茱莉亚摇了摇头。

"妈妈，我不愿意，练舞蹈太疼了，我不适合。我想好好学习，想去更多的地方，我们回家吧。"

母亲认真的看着茱莉亚。

　　"是真的吗？妈妈没有骗你，你要是真的喜欢，无论你选择什么路，妈妈都会陪着你。"

　　"妈妈，是真的，我真的不想永远跳舞，我想好好学习，碾压掉他们。"她指的是在学校的几个学习上的竞争对手。

　　母亲很欣慰地抱了抱女儿，回过头来对塞亚琳说："我没什么好选择的，自从茱莉亚出生起，我就知道我这辈子的任务是守护好我的女儿，只要女儿想要的，我全力给予她，并且陪伴她，这就是我的人生任务，所以，我们选择回到原来的地方，尽管那里并不完美，充满肮脏的人性和激烈的竞争，可是我的孩子，她需要拥有完整的人生，去真正的人群中厮杀，像您的祖先一样，为自己的'王冠'赢得荣耀和尊敬，所以哪怕前程困难重重，我们都得回去，那是女儿和我的战场。"

　　塞亚琳满眼洋溢着自豪，欣慰地看着母亲说：

　　"令人尊敬的母亲，您和女儿会实现你们所想，我会派鹏鸟安全护送你们回家。"

　　三人分别感谢了塞亚琳后，只见墙壁上的屏幕画面突然转换，变成了火车站模样，旋即墙壁从中间分开，开出了一辆小轿车，开车者正是菜场经常和茱莉亚母亲攀谈的大妈，两人友好地同菜场大妈打好招呼后，便跟随菜场大妈上了轿车。大妈一路沿着地下堡垒的通道一路开，茱莉亚看着前方乌漆麻黑的路，以及明晃晃的车灯留下的唯一亮光，一切都像刚来的那天所发生的，空气安静的只剩车的引擎声，自己和母亲坐在车里，好像被全世界抛弃了。她看着周围，想着人生许就是这样，开始便是结局，结局也是开始，所以离别相聚都要习以为常。

"一会儿你们坐上'鹏鸟'，也就是老板的小型私人飞机，要牢牢遵守规矩。"开车的菜场大妈说。

"什么规矩？"茱莉亚问。

**"向前飞的时候，不要向下看；向上飞的时候，不要向下瞧。**不然一切都很容易前功尽弃。"

"好的。"母女两人应着。

菜场大妈从后视镜里给了茱莉亚一个微笑。

向前飞不要向下看，向上飞不要向后瞧，默念着这两句，在'鹏鸟'的护送下，母女二人回到了家乡小镇。虽然在巴城过去了半年，可是在自己的家乡却只过了6天，一切一如往常，大家都觉得茱莉亚母女是正常出了个差。

奇怪的是，母女二人并没有如塞亚琳所说那样忘掉这段经历。多年后，茱莉亚时常怀疑自己是不是真的到过叫巴城的地方，一个巴掌大的小城，那里的人民亲切友好，山清水秀，瓜香果甜，那里的女人毫无压力，她们只为了自己而美丽，只为了热爱而跳舞。那里的日子幸福的如梦幻泡影，人们毫无竞争，只需要沉醉于理想，政府高质量提供你所需要的一切。这样的日子，有的人想要留下来，有的人却想要逃离出去。

茱莉亚回来了，她很清楚自己的内心选择，知道自己的任务还没有完成，虽然在巴城以外的地方，总是波折，总是阴冷，也总是压力许多，但这是完整自己人生的必经之路。

　　未经磨难的人生，又如何能够去全然体会幸福呢？这是茱莉亚总结到的，因为在巴城后面的两个月里，她已经有些感到无聊了，那样的日子，似乎更适合身体已经逐渐失去了行动力的老年人，怪不得，巴城留下的人年纪也都比较大了。而作为年轻人，在这波澜壮阔的人生丛林里窜梭前行，受伤愈合，是完整人生的一部分。

**我们总想逃离苦难、伤害、未知，却不知这些都是幸福的一部分，有的人只想要快乐，可是没有了痛苦，也就无所谓快乐，两者一起，才真正组成幸福的人生。**

Printed in Great Britain
by Amazon

36164786R00090